# An Innocent Co-Ed

Toriano Bohanna

# CHAPTER ONE

At the moment, the seat by Joe Brown's side was empty and Joe hoped it would stay that way. Joe had spent a lot of time on during the last few years and he inevitably dreamed about having some beautiful friendly young chick get on board at the last minute and find no seat vacant except the one next to him. One thing would lead to another and after a long intimate conversation, they would head for the nearest hotel the moment the bus arrived at the station.

Unfortunately, it never seemed to happen and he had ceased to believe that the beautiful young chick would ever materialize and rather than try to communicate with someone boring, he preferred to be alone with his thoughts. The young man had been through a lot in the past few years and had been forced to grow up very abruptly. He had wanted to go to the university but he had not been able to afford it, so he had signed on board a freighter bound for South America hoping that eventually he would be able to save enough money to go back home and go to school. Well, here he was, three years later, older, richer and more experienced.

The young ex-sailor grinned to himself as he thought of the girls he had met in all the ports his ship had docked in. Oh, it had been fun at first, but after awhile they had all begun to look alike and he and his friends had even given up all hope of anything but straight forward unfriendly sex, despite the fact that some of the girls had learned to speak English reasonably well and he himself had mastered quite a few phrases in Spanish and Portuguese. But somehow, there had never been time for anything. On their few days of leave away from the ship, they had gotten into the habit of grabbing the first whore they could find, throwing her on her back and driving into her stomach without so much as a moment's foreplay, taking out their aggressions and hatred on the small, perfectly-formed bodies of these lithe, slender Indian and Spanish women.

Most of the girls he had, known in South America had been tired and uninteresting, selling their bodies for money and nothing more, and there had been a vulgar saying among the sailor's: Anyone who fucks a South American is too lazy to jack off!

But every so often, Joe had succeeded in finding a girl who still enjoyed her work at least a little and would take the trouble to put some effort into what she was doing. And these "special" girls had managed to convince him that a female South American knew more about love-making by the time she was eighteen than an American woman would ever learn.

Joe's penis jerked slightly in his pants as he recalled the last night he had spent in Aruba just before shipping out for the States and his final trip on the ship. He had gone to visit a girl whom he had begun to see rather regularly during his off duty hours, hoping she would be available to entertain him on his last night in town. The young girl was a whore, pure and simple, but she loved fucking better than anyone else in the world and the young sailor had always found her perfectly happy to indulge any obscene desire he might have.

As he walked in that last day, the girl had flown into his arms without a word, pressing her lithe, high-breasted body against him and pulled him urgently towards the bed. His sweat-soaked clothes had fallen off with fantastic speed and a moment later he had found himself as naked as she, lying on top of her softly yielding body, her firm little bud-like nipples boring into his chest. The pretty young Aruban prostitute had thrust her thigh high up into his loins as they writhed around on the narrow bed, bringing his already-stimulated cock to an almost unbearable state of throbbing hardness. It had been almost a month since he had last enjoyed a woman, and Joe could feel that the moisture was already seeping from the glands at the end of his long lust-thickened shaft, trapped between the soft surfaces of her tightly-clasped thighs.

"Oh, fuck me," she had murmured hotly. "Fuck me good!"

Then the tawny-skinned girl had massaged him with delicate, experienced fingers, stroking the red, blood-swollen tip of his cock until the young man was afraid he was going to explode, cumming all over the soft flat plane of her stomach even before he had gotten a chance to worm his thickly pulsing instrument up into the hidden recesses of her lust-inspiring body.

"I'm going home soon," he had whispered to her. "Let's make this one extra good."

"I will show you some things to teach the girls in America," she had promised in return. "I have heard your women do not know how to make love. Lie on your back, please."

Joe had obediently rolled over, knowing what she was going to do to him and enjoying it in advance as he looked down at her expectantly. The brown skinned, black-eyed girl had then crouched slavishly between his knees, stroking his cock with her hand and sliding the loose foreskin up and down over the muscular super-hardened shaft until Joe was sure he was going to lose his mind. Her face had hovered above him, only a few inches above the throbbing moist head of his cock, and the young sailor had discovered in that moment that his hips were possessed of a will of their own, rising and falling rhythmically as she massaged him.

A broad, man-pleasing grin had crossed her face then as she dropped her head slowly and torturously, her tongue flicking teasingly into the dampness of the hard pulsating gland, and this extremely erotic stimulation had forced a low groan of pleasure to the lips of the young sailor.

Soon, the crucial moment had arrived. While Joe had looked down with unconcealed ecstasy, the Aruban girl had closed her soft red lips around the sensitive head of his cock, her tongue lapping obscenely back and forth as she trapped the huge bulbous tip of his penis inside the moist warm cavern of her mouth. Joe had never had anything quite like this before in his young life, and he had looked down in amazement at the sight of his long hard shaft of flesh stuck luridly up into her tightly ovaled mouth while the girls had sucked on him like a mad-woman, using her hands to play with the soft, sensitive skin of his testicles. As she had slavered submissively over him, Joe had enjoyed the lashings of her tongue as she had twirled it maddeningly around the tiny opening of the involuntarily jerking gland at the end of his long heavily swollen penis. The wildly pleasurable sensations she was creating in his loins were mind-blowing to say the least, and the sight of her crouched over him like a slave made it all the better.

Somehow the girl had sensed that Joe was turning on powerfully by now, and she had worked like a demon to make him cum, laboring obscenely to force him to shoot off into her mouth, spewing the great steaming streams of white creamy semen into the depths of her willing throat. Enormous swirling sensations of heated desire had started to build up deep inside of him by this point, and the young sailor had realized that she was driving him inexorably towards the most powerful orgasm of his life. The muscles of his flat hard stomach had gone completely rigid and he had observed with lewd delight the tiny droplets of saliva oozing from the corners of her cock-stuffed mouth.

Then suddenly he had gasped as the spasm swept uncontrollably over him. His moment had arrived and he seized her head in a vise-like grip as he felt the white-hot cum begin its final charge from the repository in his aching sperm-bloated balls out through the wildly contracting channel of his penis and into the sanctuary of her madly-sucking mouth. Still watching the bent over prostitute like a hawk, Joe had seen her cheeks billow out like a balloon as her mouth was suddenly filled with the warm sensuous fluid, and he had expected her to stop immediately to spit out this lewd choking mixture of cum and saliva.

But instead, the girl had absolutely reveled in her masochistic debasement, gulping his obscene male cum as if it were the nectar of the gods. Even as his cock slowly wilted, she had continued to suck gently on him, never letting up on her efforts until she had brought his tingling penis back to its fully erected state. Then she had collapsed back on the bed, her legs sprayed lasciviously apart, inviting him to fuck her in the usual way.

Much later that night, when Joe had dressed to leave, the girl had cried a little and unexpectedly dropped to her knees in front of him as he had been counting out the usual payment with a little bit extra as a farewell present. She had removed his now exhausted cock from his pants one last time, kissed it with open-mouthed passion, and then slipped the money back into his pocket.

His last night in Aruba had been on the house!

The bus jolted to a stop and Joe Brown shook his head to drive away this mixed bag of recollections. For him, South America and her people were things of the past, to be forgotten if possible. He was a little long in the tooth to be starting college at the age of twenty-five, but the money he had saved from his jobs on ships over the years was going to pay his way. He had worked so hard just for this reason and now he had just enough money to make it through the four years he needed. And the added maturity and worldliness which came from his traveles and experiences should give him some advantages as far as the college girls were concerned. Joe had heard that most of these coeds were pretty wild, and a man no longer needed to visit a prostitute to get his rocks off; all you had to do was walk across the campus! Joe was perfectly serious about getting a good education, but he saw no reason why he couldn't enjoy himself while he was at it.

Then suddenly, the miracle happened! The door to the bus opened and in walked a girl, struggling with an assortment of handbags. Joe Brown sat back happily and gave his eyes a treat. She was about nineteen, and moved with the unconscious grace of a woman too young to have realized clearly how beautiful she was or what kind of an effect she had upon men. The newcomer to the car was a brunette, rather tall, and as she strained to move her cumbersome baggage down the narrow aisle, Joe could see that her sweater-covered breasts were unusually heavy and sensuous, swaying temptingly as she turned her voluptuously curved body. Her hips were narrow and well-formed and the short skirt she wore cut alluringly across her milk-white tapered thighs nearly a foot above her knees.

Joe shook his head in wonderment. Girls like this normally traveled with an escort or a parent. With a body and a face like that, it really was not wise for her to make a long journey like this alone!

Naturally, she would go and sit next to someone else. Brown knew better than to expect two miracles during the same bus ride, and he watched anxiously as her eyes swept the car, searching for an empty seat. Seeing the one next to him, she headed toward the amazed young ex-sailor who leaped instantly to his feet to help her with her bags.

"Hi!" she chirped in a friendly tone. "I'm Melanie Abbott."

"Hello," he responded somewhat more formally. "Are you going to Dallas?"

"Yes, I'm going to be a freshman at the University there. Isn't it exciting?"

Given the fact that several hundred thousand young teenagers rushed off somewhere every year to become freshmen, there was no particular reason why her announcement should be remarkable, but the girl's fresh innocent enthusiasm was contagious and Joe found himself confessing that he too was enrolling as a first year student, and before long the two new students were busily discussing the courses they intended to take.

Melanie vaguely recalled having been told by her parents that proper young ladies did not start conversations with strangers on buses or other public places, but after all, this young man seemed so pleasant and nice, not to mention the fact that he was a student like her. Joe explained the job he had been on for the past few years, and it gave her a warm safe feeling to be sitting next to an older, more experienced person, someone who could guide her if she needed advice. Not that anything bad was likely to happen, of course. According to a tourist book she had read, Dallas was a happy friendly city. She had looked at the brouchure published by the University and had scanned pages photographs showing happy healthy young people playing at sports or busily studying with smiles on their faces. Oh, there was no question about it! This was going to be the best experience of her life!

"Are you going to take English 1A?" inquired the ex-sailor, leafing through a university catalog.

"Yes, are you? That would be wonderful. We could sit together!" she gushed, without thinking of how her remark must have sounded. "I love English. I made good grades in it in high school, too."

Of course, life was not always going to be peaches and cream, Melanie reminded herself, and who knew what the future could bring? She had, for example, had her appendix out when she was eighteen, a most unpleasant experience, and then more recently, there had been the nasty business with Tony....

Melanie shifted uncomfortably in her seat, noticing that the old bus seemed to be vibrating a lot, and firmly resolving that she would not start day-dreaming about her last date with Tony again. It was over and done with, she insisted to herself. There was no reason to keep worrying about it, but unfortunately, Joe seemed to be busily studying his catalog and there was no light conversation to distract, her.

And it kept coming back to her, like the nightmare it had been. Tony had been her steady boyfriend throughout high school and the two of them had made quite a pair. The King and the Queen, their friends had called them, since he had excelled at all forms of sports, and she had always been considered the most attractive young lady in town. Tony's father was one of the wealthiest men in the state and his son was normally on his best behavior all of the time, but there were nights.....

There were nights when Tony was allowed to borrow his father's Cadillac to take her to a school dance or to a movie downtown. On his way home, the young man would normally suggest a "quiet chat" before turning in, and drive a few miles out of town to some secluded spot where the Highway patrol were not likely to harass them. Sex had never been really discussed in the Abbott home, but Melanie always had an uncomfortable feeling that she should not permit Tony to caress her ripe succulent breasts the way he liked to do, but she had heard that all the other girls at school permitted this and a lot more besides and she was anxious not to seem unsophisticated or childish about these things.

Some nights, Tony's hands had roamed even farther than usual and she had told him to stop, knowing that this was definitely a violation of the strict moral code her family had been pounding into her for so many years. Her mother particularly was something of a fanatic as far as religion was concerned and had always made it a point to send her to church every Sunday, ran or shine, and had warned her repeatedly about "impure acts" without ever giving her daughter a concrete idea of precisely what she meant by this vague term.

Liquor was another evil thing as far as Melanie's parents were concerned, and consequently the girl had never had too much to do with it until the night of the graduation party when she and Tony had very definitely had too much "punch" to drink. Afterwards, during their "quiet chat" in the countryside, she had relaxed in the soft cushioned back seat of the big luxurious car, her head pleasantly spinning with whiskey, and allowed her boyfriend to excite her with long penetrating kisses and to gradually unzip the back of her dress and unfasten the snap on her brassiere. She had told herself quite clearly that this was evil, but in actual fact, the thing had been too tight all evening and her heavy womanly breasts tumbled free of their restrictive confinement, making her sigh with real physical relief.

Capitalizing on her drunken confusion, her eager young boyfriend had placed his hands directly on the naked tender skin of her heavily rounded breasts, massaging the tiny brown nipples until they became hard and turgid, something which had never happened to her before. Other strange things were going on at the same time, and Melanie had shifted uneasily on the smooth fabric of the back seat, feeling an unfamiliar tingling sensation begin to build up in the base of her stomach, no it was even lower than that, it was down in the area between her legs and the tingling was causing her hips to shake back and forth as if she were trying to scratch an unusually persistant itch. She had been innocently deciding that it was the punch which was causing these strange reactions, when Tony had further complicated matters by lowering his head abruptly and fastening his greedy lips over one swollenly trembling nipple which he began to suck.

The sensation had been perfectly maddening, but the girl had had no prior experience with this bold and direct kind of sexual excitement, and she was too naive to realize that she was becoming powerfully stimulated by all the depraved things her boyfriend was doing to her. She had tried to consider the matter logically, wondering how far she could afford to let him go before it would be necessary to tell him very sternly that he had to stop.

But while she was pondering the matter, Tony had escalated the situation by slipping his hand directly up under her long skirt, pushing the dress far up over her cream-like white thighs. The dazzled young girl had been so occupied with what he was doing with the highly-sensitive bud-like little nipples on her breasts that she hardly noticed this new intrusion at first. Tony had made the most of his opportunity, plunging his obscenely probing fingers all. the way up past the tops of her nylon stockings and running his fingers lasciviously over the surface of her panties, causing a lewd pressure to the tingling "vee" of her virginal pussy.

"Oh no, Tony, please...." she had mumbled piteously, but the young athlete was now too powerfully aroused to remember his manners and he had pressed on with this indecent invasion, inserting his middle finger up underneath the elastic legband of her white cotton panties, and running it up into the soft moist pubic hair surrounding the tightly-closed lips of her hither-to-unpenetrated vagina. Accidentally, the tip of his maurauding finger had then brushed against the tiny pink button of her clitoris and an electric shock had raced immediately through her sensitive inexperienced body, forcing a moan involuntarily from her lips.

"Oh, my God," she had gasped, unable to believe that this was actually happening to a nice girl like her. "This is ... is what married people do, Tony! We mustn't!"

But Tony had ignored her. His own knowledge of sex was limited to what he had heard in locker-room discussions with the other male students, but he had realized that his girl was both fairly drunk and really stimulated, a situation worth pursuing. He had pushed harder, getting a few more fingers into the moist warm hair of her unresisting pussy and his middle finger had actually succeeded in penetrating past the quivering wet lips of her vagina. The obscenely impaled girl had wiggled desperately around on his hand, half wanting him to stop immediately, and half hoping he would go on like this forever, digging his sharp white teeth into the soft flaccid flesh of her breasts and stroking the glistening moistened nerve-endings of her pulsating little clitoris with his finger, until something happened to relieve the gnawing hungering sensation which was steadily building up inside of her trembling overexcited young body.

The next sound she had heard was the metallic rasp of a zipper being opened and with a shock, she had realized that Tony was undoing the front of his pants. She had studied about the male reproductive organ in biology class, and had a vague idea of how it was supposed to work, but naturally, she had never seen one before and somehow she had decided that this would all be less sinful if she did not see one now.

She got her eyes closed just in time, but the lust-driven young athlete had had no intention of letting her off that easily. With his free arm, he had guided her shaking hand down to the hardness of his rigidly erected cock and wrapped her fingers firmly around the long heavy shaft. Melanie's mind went into orbit. It had never occurred to her that a penis could be so large, so hard, so long! As she touched him, Tony had thrust his fingers even farther into her slowly-expanding little vaginal hole, and for a moment, absolutely intensive pleasure had flooded her entire body, causing her instinctively to squeeze his penis. Without knowing exactly what she was doing or why, the young girl had begun to message the thick leathery foreskin of his massive instrument, moving up and down firmly and forcing groan after groan to his lips.

The sexual thrills had started bombarding her intensively now and her staggered, alcohol-numbed mind had been too full of pleasure to allow for rational thought; without thinking, she had slowly allowed her thighs to separate, relaxing the muscles in her finely-tapered legs to give him even greater access to the mysteries of her moistly palpitating vagina. Melanie had not understood precisely what was happening at the time, but the orgiastic juices from deep inside her over-stimulated body were starting to flow and she could feel the moisture seeping slowly down between her legs and into the narrowly twisted-aside crotchband of her panties, wetting his hand and her dress beneath.

Then, suddenly, Tony had lost control and tried to roll on top of her, slipping his knee in between her widely-spread legs and trying to thrust his lust-thickened cock into the narrow wet cuntal opening now occupied by his fingers. Instinctively, she had fought back, clawing at him like a cornered animal and twisting violently back and forth to avoid the menacing cudgel of his penis.

He had succeeded in forcing the blunt, blood-engorged tip of his cock up beneath the elastic fibre of her panties when unexpectedly it had all happened. Groaning as if he had been wounded, the hard-bodied athlete had collapsed on top of her writhing and twisting young body and she had felt a steaming jet of hot sticky fluid spray into the warm tangle of her unprotected pubic hair, drenching the open vulnerable lips of her cunt and dripping obscenely down onto her dress.

And that had been the end of it. As if he were angry at something, Tony had pulled himself away from her, mumbling something about a "cock-teaser", rapidly adjusting his clothing and peering apprehensively out the window to make sure they had not been observed. Whimpering with fear and unhappiness, Melanie had used the hankie in her purse to wipe away the warm pungent cum from her nakedly exposed skin, and then struggled back into the confinement of her brassiere.

As soon as she was decent, Tony had hurled himself into the front seat and had driven her rapidly home without saying another word. A few minutes later, she had found herself alone on the sidewalk in front of her house, wondering what all of this could possibly have meant.

\* \* \*

"Oh, were you sleeping?"

"Uh...? Oh, I guess I was just day-dreaming," Melanie stammered, blushing up to her ear-lobes, as if the young ex-sailor next to her had somehow been able to read her mind.

"I just asked you if you'd done much traveling before," Joe continued, wondering what had brought on her sudden embarrassment and trying to get the conversation rolling again. By a stroke of sheer good fortune, he had found this gorgeous creature before the other men on campus had laid eyes on her, and he wanted to capitalize on his advantage while it lasted. Naturally he realized that this was not the kind of gal he could expect to take to bed after the first date. She looked distinctly on the innocent side, possibly even-horror of horrors-a virgin, and it would take a little of the flowers and candy treatment to bring her around. But unless this were a very exceptional campus, she was going to be the best looking woman at the university, and Joe knew he had to cement their relationship while he could.

"Yes," Melanie finally got her wits together enough to answer his question. "Daddy and Mamma took me to England two years ago and Germany the year before that. But really I haven't seen too much of the United States. Have you traveled a lot?"

"Oh, I've knocked around the States enough," admitted Joe casually, making an effort to sound like a sophisticated man of the world. "And while I was on the ship in South America, I got to see a lot of the country-side and spend a couple of days in the Carribean."

"Oh, how interesting, I've always wanted to see South America, you know, the Incas and Aztec's ruins, and everything. But it must have been lonesome for you, so far away from home?"

"Well, I met a lot of good friends down there, but for female companionship, we were up a creek. My shipmates had to make do with the pros."

"What's a pro?"

xi

Joe looked at her for a moment to make sure she was not kidding him, but quickly realized that the girl was even more innocent than he had imagined.

"A Prostitute," he explained nonchalantly. "Some of them had learned quite a lot of English in bed and I met one or two who had first-class minds, as well as pretty interesting bodies."

"Oh, prostitutes," whispered Melanie, shocked that such a nice young man would lower himself to associate with such terrible people, and feeling her blush return at the same time, "I've heard my father talking about them, although naturally we don't have any in my home town. He saw one once in Boston."

"Was she any good?"

"Oh no, I don't mean that he ... you know ... went with her or anything. He just saw her on the street," stumbled Melanie, now more embarrassed than ever, but not wanting to appear like an unsophisticated hick in front of this obviously-experienced young man. "Weren't you afraid ... you know ... of getting some kind of a disease by ... uh, spending your time with those girls?"

"Honey, you don't get syph from spending time with prostitutes, you get it by making love to them, and I did, but thanks to the wonders of penicillin, I was out of the woods in no time at all."

Melanie was a little startled at the idea of sitting next to a man who had actually been in bed with a prostitute and suddenly she gazed at him and found herself imagining what he looked like naked, wondering if his "thing" was as big as Tony's monstrous penis that she had held in her hand that night. She was instantly ashamed of this obscene thought and could feel her face turning the color of a fire truck.

"Hey, you look pretty when you blush," Joe kidded her. "If talking about prostitutes embarrasses you, we could talk about something else."

Now he's treating me like a child, Melanie thought, angry at herself for having revealed her innocence.

"No, not in the slightest," she replied, giving him a little of her finishing school voice. "I assure you that I am quite sophisticated about these things. In fact, my friends all know how hard it is to shock me."

"Really," responded the ex-sailor, immediately deciding to pick up the challenge and knowing that some girls got turned on by a little rough talk. "I would say just from looking at you that you're a typical small-town virgin."

"Why, how dare you say a thing like that!" she hissed at him, dreadfully afraid that the other passengers would overhear this lurid conversation.

"Well, are you?"

"Oh ... I'm not sure. ... I mean, No! No! I mean Yes!" she babbled, realizing that she was making a perfect fool of herself. In actual fact, Melanie was not totally sure in her own mind whether she could truthfully claim to be a virgin or not. The night of the "incident" with Tony, he had been digging his fingers cruelly into her unused little cunt, and even though he had never quite succeeded in penetrating her with his rigid lust-hardened penis, there had been traces of blood on her legs when she had inspected herself in the bathroom that night, and she had been worrying ever since that he might have pierced the thin delicate membrane of her hymen with his cruelly invading fingers.

"Now, would you like to explain what all that was supposed to mean," Joe laughed, unable to believe that anyone as good-looking and sexually desirable as Melanie could possibly be uncertain about the exact status of her virginity.

"I've done a great deal of horseback riding," the embarrassed girl explained, avoiding his eyes and pulling away from him in the seat, having remembered just in time that girls who rode a lot sometimes lost their virginity naturally that way. "And anyway, I don't see how my virginity is any of your business!"

"No, I suppose it isn't, honey, and I'm sorry if I pissed you ... I mean, if I offended you, but you know, the fact is, I'm a little worried about you."

"I see no reason why you should be! An hour's conversation doesn't make me your girl friend!"

"I guess it doesn't, although I hope you'll give me the chance to work on that as well," Joe continued, looking at her seriously. "No, what worries me is the fact that you look a little innocent to be wandering around Dallas alone. This is a big bad city, honey."

"Are you suggesting I'm not capable of looking after myself?"

"Yeah, more or less," Joe admitted, lighting a cigarette and offering her one. The girl hesitated, then accepted his peace offering, leaning forward to allow him to light it for her.

"Now, for example, if a guy offered you a cigarette and it was rolleed by hand, would you take it?"

Melanie considered. Her parents disapproved of her smoking, but they did it themselves and the girl had learned to enjoy an occasional puff.

"Yes, I suppose I would, if he were a nice boy who didn't keep asking me about my virginity. What difference does it make how it was rolled?"

"Well now, Melanie, honey, have you ever learned about marijuana?"

"Of course! It's a drug and I hear it's harmless."

"Maybe it is and maybe it isn't," Joe replied slowly. "The point is that it does funny things to your head. Now a guy who finds a chick as naive as you are is liable to slip you one and then try some funny stuff."

"Not a chance. I never go around with that kind of a person."

"Okay, okay, have it your way," he finally conceded, seeing that further argument was useless. "But look, at least let me give you a telephone number in Dallas where I can be reached. I'm staying near the campus at a friend's place and if you run into difficulties, you can give me a call and I'll come running."

"Just like the calvary!" retorted Melanie sarcastically. "I assure you I'll be quite all right. There's nothing to be afraid of in a place like Dallas."

But Joe jotted a telephone number on a slip of paper and stuffed it into her purse anyway. Too bad, he thought dejectedly. I always manage to put my foot in my mouth one way or another. She's built like a million dollars and that face could win beauty contest all by itself, but she hasn't learned which end is up yet, and that's going to land her in lots of trouble before long!

CHAPTER TWO

The two new freshmen chatted occasionally for the remainder of the trip, but the fun had gone out of their conversation somehow. It was night when they reached the bus terminal in Dallas, a dingy unpleasant place full of bums and suspicious-looking characters lounging around on benches with apparently nothing to do. Joe took one look at the scene and found his worries immediately returning. Why the hell had she worn that short skirt? Those long sleekly-tapered legs would attract attention from every man in the station and somebody was dead sure going to try something with her if she started walking around alone.

"Where are you staying tonight?" he asked, with an attempt at sounding casual.

"Oh, I'll be going over to the university woman's dormitory," Melanie assured him brightly. "Were you planning on calling to see whether I brushed my teeth before going to bed?"

"You'd better learn to read more accurately," he snapped. "It says in the catalog that the dorms don't open until the twentieth of the month, which is three days from now. What do you plan to do in the meantime?"

Melanie was thunderstruck. It had never occurred to her that there would not be a warm cozy bed waiting for her at the university as soon as she arrived.

"In that case, I'll check into a hotel," she stammered, caught a little off-guard.

"Look, why don't you let me take you over to my friend's pad. He and his girl friend live in a big place on the edge of the campus and you can sleep in the bed they were saving for me. I can flop on the couch and...."

"Oh, no you don't," Melanie reacted immediately. "That's exactly the sort of thing my parents warned me about."

"I'm glad they warned you about something," muttered the young man, but he said no more and helped the girl get her luggage down off the rack, watching the neat, smoothly rounded half-moons of her buttocks as he followed her off the bus. As he placed the bags on the ground next to the doorway, having momentarily lost sight of Melanie in the crowd, a small, seedy-looking man in a weather-beaten wrinkled suit approached with a sly lecherous grin.

"Hey buddy, like a girl for the night?" the stranger mumbled, looking furtively around him. "Your choice of the hottest babes in town!"

For a moment, Joe was tempted. It had been a long hot journey and talking to the voluptuous young coed had excited him considerably. But he rejected the idea anyway. For one thing, he had already decided that he was through with paying for it; secondly it would be a little sad to screw some tired old bag after he had been excited by someone as attractive as Melanie.

"No ... no thanks, not tonight."

"In case you change your mind, address is 16 Angelos Court. Just ask for Ruby. We get all the college crowd out there."

Joe nodded and forgot the address almost as soon as the little pimp disappeared from sight. Then he returned and found Melanie at his elbow.

"Well, see you around the campus, as they say," she smiled at him, offering her hand.

"Yeah, see you in English. Remember, you promised to sit next to me. Hey, there's a cab for you!"

\* \* \*

What a stroke of good fortune, Melanie congratulated herself as she stepped into the back seat of the taxi. If I hadn't over-heard that man giving Joe the address of a hotel where all the college kids go, I don't know what I'd done.

"Where to, Miss?" inquired the taxi-driver, greedily eyeing her lust-inciting figure through the rear view mirror.

"Ruby's," she told him brightly. "16 Angelos Court."

The taxi driver's jaw dropped open, but he wisely decided to say nothing. About time these college girls stopped giving it away for free, he thought savagely, and the cab roared off into the night.

\* \* \*

One expects a woman who makes a career of running a brothel to look at least a little like a madam, but in fact, Ruby presented the appearance of being someone's grandmother rather than anything as sinister as the propretress of a house of ill repute. As she sat talking with Gerome, her combination bouncer and business manager, she looked positively saintly, her gentle black hair streaked with grey, and it was well groomed and her slightly-spreading matronly figure neatly covered by a sober black dress.

Gerome, on the other hand, looked exactly like what he was: a man with a long criminal past who had spent most of the forty years of his life pursuing all the vices of mankind and inventing a few of his own along the way. Enormously powerful, he towered at least a foot over the head of his dainty female boss, but seemed to respect her at least as an equal. With blonde, almost white bushy eyebrows and a sports shirt left open in front to display his rippling chest muscles, Gerome looked about as mean as he was.

"It's this immorality," he was complaining. "Why don't the churches get on the job and teach the people the difference between right and wrong?"

"Oh, it's a new age, Gerome," agreed the pleasant-looking old woman. "In the good old days, when a man needed some real fun in the sack, he had to come to us, because unmarried girls didn't do certain things and proper wives didn't behave like whores in bed with their husbands. But it's all changed, Gerome. Nowadays, these kids have their first period and they head for a drug store to buy a bottle of birth control pills. And these wives! They sit around reading books on how to entertain a man in bed. No wonder the boys don't come to see us anymore. They're getting all the action they can handle at home!"

"It's disgraceful," asserted Gerome and Ruby nodded in agreement. "Morals are shot to hell. And theese college girls are the worst of all."

"Ah, remember the good old days," reminised the older woman nostalgically. "Remember Gerome, on a Saturday night, how we used to get professors, important businessmen, real cultured people. Why I can recall when I wouldn't open the door to anyone who wasn't wearing a tie!"

Gerome leaned forward to pour another dash of cognac into Ruby's teacup and then tilted the bottle back to take a long swig himself.

"Nowadays, we get nuttin' but perverts," he grumbled. "Them freaky guys with whips and chains and bull shit like that. And most of 'em are more ignorant than me, and that's sayin' something."

"Our girls are getting older too," observed the dark haired woman. "That makes a difference too. Gila's been with us for eighteen years now. Most men like something young and a little fresh, I'm afraid."

"And unwilling! Ruby, I'll tell you something, free sex is so available these days that a lot of guys only get turned on if they can take a gal who doesn't wanna. Maybe we could get one of the broads to pretend she's a white slave captive or something."

"Wouldn't sell," decided Ruby after a moment of consideration. "Everybody knows our gals will do anything for a buck. How about hiring a new girl? Maybe get an oriental chick from someplace and tell the clients she's a slave? Some of the guys would dig that kind of thing...."

"Nan, a whore looks like a whore, no matter how young she is. I wonder if we could get a broad who really wasn't a whore ... y'know, grab somebody and lock'er up in the 'special room.'"

"Yeah, sure," retorted Ruby sarcastically. "And how you gonna get some chick to walk in here? But we got to do something or go out of business, that's for sure."

"Right! I'm too old to go back into second-story work, and selling pot just doesn't bring in enough dough. If I could break into the university market, I'd be a millionaire, but those damn college boys take one look at me and run the other way. Maybe I should let me hair grow or something."

The doorbell rang unexpectedly and the two jaded merchants of human flesh looked up at each other in surprise.

"That couldn't be a customer," commented Ruby dubiously. "Are any of the girls sober enough to work?"

"Yeah, but if they ain't, I'll send the John in to you," joked Gerome, moving his massive body towards the door.

"Good evening, Sir," came Melanie Abbott's light refined voice. "Is this Ruby's?"

For a second, the burly bouncer simply struggled to find his voice, his widened eyes roaming lustfully over the girl's splendidly-formed young body. Finally, his mind boggling at the sight of her, he managed to croak out an answer.

"Might be. What kin we do for you?"

"I'd like a room for the night," explained the girl brightly. "I hear that all the university crowd comes here."

Gerome could not be considered in any way an intelligent man but four decades in the underworld had made him as crafty and cunning as a forest animal. After a moment's hesitation, he understood that some kind of mistake was happening before his very eyes, and an instant later his mind was at work, planning ways he could turn the situation to some devious advantage.

"Why of course, Miss," he responded, stepping quickly outside to pick up the girl's two bulging suitcases. "Most of the cultured folks in Dallas come here 'cause our atmosphere is kinda extra-refined. Would you step this way, please?"

Gerome led the tall lithe brunette into the lobby, hoping desperately that one of the whores would not take it into her mind to wander into the room half-naked just at that point.

"Who is it, Gerome?" called Ruby from her office, her voice sounding sweet and grandmotherly as always. "Is it a John?"

"Melanie was frankly happy to hear a woman's voice because this ferocious-looking man was frightening the daylights out of her. Of course he was obviously nothing more than a respectable hotel keeper, but he looked to her like a cross between a sex-maniac and a gorilla, combining the worst features of both.

"No, Ma'am," Gerome answered. "John called to say that he couldn't come this evening. It's a young lady from the university who needs a room for the night."

"Who ...?" muttered the brothel-keeper, coming to the door with her teacup in hand, but Gerome sent her a warning glance before she could give the game away.

"Oh ... well, glad to have you, Miss," she said, her experienced eyes skipping rapidly over Melanies voluptuously curved figure and the finely-tapered legs only practically concealed by her inadequate short shirt. "I think you'll find our ... uh ... accomodations modest but comfortable."

"OH, I'm sure I will," answered Melanie, looking a little dubious as she surveyed the worn furniture and cobwebs on the ceiling. Oh, it's all right, she was trying to reassure herself. I'm going to have to get used to roughing it if I expect to live on my budget. "Are there some other students staying here tonight?"

"Oh, the place is almost full," Gerome assured her, winking covertly at Ruby. "Only they are all upstairs studying their Greek. You'll see'm later on.

"Why don't we let the young lady relax on the couch for a moment, Mr. Gerome?" suggested Ruby craftily, giving her assistant a glare. "While you and I decide which room is most suitable."

Melanie seated herself uncertainly on the soiled old sofa while the bouncer followed his boss into the main office, bracing himself for the bawling-out he knew he was due to receive.

"And what on earth do you think you're doing!" she hissed at him the moment they were alone.

"Now calm down, Ruby," the big brute answered her. "I'm not doing nothing. At least we kin make a couple of bucks by renting a room for the night. An' I got a couple of ideas, but I gotta do some thinkin' first."

"Gerome, that little broad has got class written all over her," snapped the whore house owner.

"We mess around with her and we could have troubles with the law."

"And who knows she's here?" countered the bouncer. "Nobody! Ruby, just leave everything to me.

And without waiting for permission, the bulky muscular man wheeled quickly out of the office before the older woman could think of any further objections.

"Right this way, young lady," Gerome boomed, sweeping her bags up off the floor as if they were filled with feathers and then barging up a narrow, poorly lit flight of stairs. Melanie followed, some of her fears returning as they left the sanctuary of the living room and the reassuring presence of the kindly white-haired woman.

Gerome knew precisely where he was headed and he moved as fast as his legs would carry him, still fearful that one of his whores would chose precisely this moment to leave her room and ruin his charade. Fortunately for his evil intentions, however, he managed to sneak his unsuspecting victim into the "special" room at the end of the corridor before she could see any evidence that this was not just another run-down hotel. The room was "special" since Ruby had had it specially built many years before, putting in sound-proofing and a two-way mirror for patrons with rather peculiar tastes. In this room, a whore and her customer could make as much noise as they pleased without fear of being overheard. And to double the fun, others could watch without being seen themselves from a hidden compartment concealed behind the mirror. Many a sordid orgy had been staged in the "special" room, and Gerome was hoping that he could arrange at least one more.

"I think this will be real comfy, Miss," he announced, switching on a light and gesturing around the room.

Actually, Melanie was pleasantly surprised. The rest of the hotel had seemed rather grimy, but this room was quite neat and pleasant. The bed was double and looked soft and inviting and the bathroom was surprisingly clean.

"I think this will do very nicely," she informed Gerome with a smile. "There's more than enough room for me here." The inexperienced young girl was unsure whether she should offer the man a tip as she had seen her father do during their travels, but in any event, Gerome did not seem immediately disposed to leave her alone, instead seating himself comfortably on a chair.

"Yes, this is our nicest room, I think," he commented, his deep gravelly voice resounding unnaturally in the soundproof room. "Most of the boys and girls from the college stay here at one time or another. A lot of em come to me for advice about their studies."

Melanie found this difficult to believe, since Gerome did not sound precisely like a man of profound learning, but she supposed that he had acquired a certain amount of rough wisdom in his life, and it was refreshing to know that he was concerned about the welfare of young people. It just goes to show you how people can't be judged by external appearances, she reminded herself, sitting down on the bed and crossing her legs.

"Would you care for a cigarette?" offered the man, extending a pack in her direction. Melanie nodded, deciding that a smoke would relax her before sleep and put it between her lips as Gerome leaned forward with a match. The taste was strong and strange, unlike anything else she had ever smoked, and her eyes widened with surprise as she observed that the cigarette was hand-rolled and remembered what Joe had said on the bus.

The bouncer followed her glance, his agile mind immediately ready with an explanation.

"Ya like 'em?" he asked solicitiously. "They're a special brand made by hand in Mexico. I got to like 'em when I was down there a few years back, working for the government."

"Oh, how fascinating it must have been!" answered the naive girl with a sigh of relief. The moment she had seen that the cigarette was manufactured by hand, she had immediately recalled Joe's warnings about marijuana, that drug that made you do silly things. But it was clear by now that Mr. Gerome was not that kind of person and he was hardly the hippie type. And naturally, the kindly old woman downstairs would hardly permit any such goings on in her hotel.

"Ya like, the taste?" asked Gerome, inhaling deeply on his own cigarette and then blowing out a cloud of smoke into the room.

"Yes, it's different, but I rather enjoy it," Melanie answered truthfully, starting to wish that he would go so that she could get her clothing off and relax. As if he were reading her mind, the big man rose to his feet, smiled at her in a frieendly innocent fashion and re-opened his cigarette box.

"I'll be on my way now and let you have your beauty sleep," he announced. "I see ya like my Mexican cigarettes, so I'll leave a couple more for you to smoke." Before she could say no, he dropped two more cigarettes on the night stand next to the bed and made his exit.

A very kind man, thought Melanie dreamily, as she took another long drag on the cigarette, and felt a relaxing blissful sensation start to creep over her tired young body. Taking another puff, she stretched languidly and then stood up to get undressed.

\* \* \*

Gerome kept the hinges on the compartment door well oiled and there was not a sound as he swung it open and stepped quickly inside. The two-way mirror was clear and the big man settled contendedly on a stool to watch the young dark-haired girl leisurely strip off her clothing, stopping every minute or so to take a deep drag on his "Mexican" cigarette. To his enormous disappointment, Melanie's back was turned towards him as she undressed and headed into the bathroom. There was the sound of water running and a moment later she emerged, wearing only a flimsy translucent pink nightie which more or less covered her firmly sensuous body from the tops of her heavily swelling tantalizing breasts down to the fullness of her cream-white thighs.

Gerome smiled evilly as he saw her climb up on the big double bed and light up the second cigarette, and he observed happily that a blank faraway look was drifting into the girl's brown eyes as the mind-killing marijuana filtered into her bloodstream and began to affect her brain. Squirming down into a comfortable position, the deceived young coed allowed her body to fall back tiredly against the pillow and the short lace nightie snaked its way up over the soft brown triangular "vee" of pussy hair in her groin, exciting him enormously as he viewed the thin pink hair-lined slit running between her slightly parted thighs.

But there was much, much more to look at, and the bouncer's eyes hungrily traced the smoothly flowing contours of her hips up to the gently heaving outlines of her large pendulous breasts inadequately concealed by the frail flimsy fabric of her nightie. Melanie's breasts were unusually high-set and closely spaced, and the nipples protruded slightly, making Gerome's cock stir anxiously in his pants with excitement and anticipation.

The hardened criminal had waited a long time for an opportunity hike this! He hated these college girls anyway, hated them for being beautiful and young and free when he was mean-looking, aging and hunted by the police. He hated them because they gave their splendid lust-arousing bodies away to their hairy young boyfriends and not to him, and worst of all, they did it for free and the college boys did not need to come to whore-houses anymore, thus ruining his business.

But now his mouth was positively watering with the prospect of getting his teeth into the delicate little nipple-buds of the voluptuous kid who'd walked right into his trap; and biting them until she moaned in agony. He wanted to run his hard murderous hands lustfully over that pure young body, churning her up into a seething, writhing mass of over-stimulated female flesh, and watching with sadistic delight as she pleaded for mercy beneath him. In his long lusty career, he had known many women, most of them whores or other criminals but nothing anywhere near as sweet and delectable as this young thing was going to be!

It would only be another few minutes. Those cigarettes were loaded with the most potent marijuana money could buy, which had then been treated with an opium base for extra kick. An inexperienced girl like this would be out cold in a matter of minutes, and then he could make his move. But the time seemed to pass slowly. Gerome would not have believed it possible, but the girl was actually puffing her way placidly through the second cigarette already having abosrbed enough of the vicious drug to stone an elephant.

But eventually the marijuana had it's enevitable effect. Melanie's eyes were still half-open but her loose-jointed posture on the bed with arms outstretched and legs spread widely apart told him clearly that he could now do whatever he wanted with her. Moving with cat-like caution, Gerome let himself out of the hidden double-mirrored compartment and slipped through the corridor and into Melanie's room. Standing silently at the foot of the bed, the brothel's bouncer gazed sadistically down at the helplessly drugged young female before him. She had passed out too quickly to have switched off the bedside lamp and in the soft light Gerome viewed the interior flesh of her white tender thighs, gleaming seductively. Almost panting with lust, he feasted his bulging eyes on the softly curling black hairs surrounding the vulnerable but tightly clasped lips of her unused little vagina, imagining the pleasures which were shortly to be his.

Gerome, old boy, he addressed himself, this is going to be the best fucking of your life! You've never had anything quite like this before! From his vast criminal experience, Gerome knew that a drugged woman could still react quite normally when a man was fucking into her, despite the fact that the victim was incapable of resisting or even understanding clearly what was happening to her. And in the morning, the whole sordid affair would seem to hawe been nothing more than a bad dream.

Except, he added to himself, in the morning she'll have a belly-full of Gerome's cum. What a gas it would be if she got pregnant! That would be something to try and explain to a doctor!

The erotic tension of the situation was goading the man's penis into a turgid state of lustfully quivering rigidity as he circled hungrily around the bed, reassuring himself that she was really out cold. Feeling the heavy blood-engorged head of his penis aching with urgent desire, he adjusted his pants to ease the pressure, noticing that tiny droplets of sticky seminal fluid were already oozing from the delicate swollen gland at the end, and he finally decided to make himself completely comfortable and open his fly.

He stood next to the bed, looking down with a deep sense of criminal satisfaction at the helpless young beauty who lay unconscious before him, carefully stimulating himself even more by massaging the thick leathery foreskin back and forth over the long menacing shaft of his penis. What he held in his hand was all the "culture" a real man needed in this rough lusty city he told himself, and once he had jammed it all the way up inside that innocent young cunt, her elegant finishing school accent would make no difference at all. She would moan and cry out just like any other tortured female, and a woman lying on her back with her thighs spread apart was no different from any other woman, educated or not.

Now, confident that he could do precisely what he wanted, this tough cruel whore-master quickly dropped his clothing on the floor, fully exposing his hard turgid member which struck out frighteningly from his groin like the gun a battleship. As an afterthought, he locked the door securely from the inside, just in case Ruby started to get curious about what he was up to and decided to barge in on him.

Now everything was ready and he hovered over the big double bed, almost too excited to touch the obscenely sprawled girl for fear he would explode on the spot, spewing steaming hot spurts of milk-white cum all over her half naked young body. There was a whole exciting range of perverse and sordid possibilities available to him, so much to choose from that for the moment, the big man could not decide where to begin. He could simply stand there and continue to caress himself until he sent his sperm flying all over her lush soft breasts, the safest course, since this way there was not a chance in the world that she would ever realize what had happened to her. But the full-bodied sensuous young woman seemed too far gone now to be aware of anything, and Gerome wanted more than something to look at.

Yes, there were other choices, and he experimented mentally a little, wanting to choose the precise perversion which best suited his depraved mood at the moment. Those half-opened ruby lips were attracting his attention now and he knelt cautiously on the bed next to her flowing raven black mane of long soft hair, moving his nakedly glistening body into position until the tip of his fully erected penis wavered only inches from her dimpled chin. He knew he was taking a chance on cumming before he wanted to, but the temptation was too great to be resisted. Thrusting his hips gently in the direction of her face, he rested the hard, thickly ridged underside of his cock directly in the valley formed by her two red lips, wiggling lasciviously back and forth as he toyed with her unsuspecting mouth. The lewd viscous pre-cum was still oozing slowly from his turgid gland, and her lips quickly became moist and lubricated as he slid his lust-bloated rod of flesh cautiously back and forth against them. The dark haired girl moaned slightly in her restless sleep, and Gerome delighted as he felt the heated air from her nostrils flowing gently over the surface of his rigid cock.

Goddamn, he thought in a mounting passion, it would be great to take her right now in the mouth! But he was not totally confident that the whole business could really be managed with an unconscious girl, and so he contented himself with experimenting a little farther with another lewd game. After all, he had not yet seen her really naked!

Moving slowly, he reached down with his one free hand and took hold of the hem of Melanie's flimsy pink nightie tugging it carefully up past the tender expanse of her belly and over the mountianous twin mounds of her heavy flaccid breasts until he could see every inch of her nakedly splendid young body. Nothing that had happened to Gerome in his entire life had excited him as much as this girl at the moment.

And she was all his! He could do whatever he wanted with the girl because he could see clearly that she was beyond defending herself!

But Gerome was not quite correct in his assessment of the situation. True, Melanie, was a long way from being in full possession of her mental facilities, but she was floating in a dream world somewhere between reality and slumber, and not fully unconscious nor full unconscious. The marijuana had thoroughly warped her brain, playing tricks and games on her, and even in her dreams she realized she was somehow in bed with a man. Sometimes it was her old boyfriend, Tony, but at other times it seemed to be the young man she had encountered on the bus, Joe. For some reason she did not clearly comprehend, it was perfectly all right for them to be in bed together and everything which had been forbidden in the past was now allowed.

"It's okay," she murmured sleepily, momentarily upsetting Gerome. "J...." and her voice trailed off again as she drifted to a lower level of consciousness. It was a strange floating sensation and Melanie somehow felt totally happy and comfortable. She was aware that her own lush, desire-arousing body was almost totally naked before this man, but for some peculiar reason none of this really bothered her. Her flesh was tingling like never before and she felt superably drowsy and alive all at the same time.

There were hands on her bare, unprotected breasts but she was convinced that they were friendly hands and there was no reason to be afraid. A strange aching feeling was creeping slowly through her veins and the doped-up girl vaguely realized that she wanted something badly, but could not clearly decide what it was.

"Sorry I was mean ... on the bus ... Joe," she whispered, half opening one eye and uselessly trying to focus on the bleary indistinct figure on the bed with her. There was a faintly pleasant buzzing sensation in her head which successfully blotted out any attempts at rational thought.

Ah, she thinks I'm somebody else, Gerome laughed cruelly to himself. So much the better. So she has been mean to this Joe on the bus, Eh? Well I'll just take some revenge on Joe's behalf and he'll never be the worse for it!

As he mumbled mercilessly to himself, the sadist permitted his hands to roam lewdly over the maiden's helplessly vulnerable body, tweaking each of her tender brown little nipples into an excruciating state of hardness and grinning cruelly to himself as he watched them both pop obediently to life. Not satisfied by a long shot, he maneuvered around on all fours above her, massaging the softly yielding flesh of her belly with his hard muscular hands and then exploring down into the moist brown triangle of pubic hair guarding the entrance of the rip fleshy folds of her cunt.

Melanie writhed with unconscious pleasure as his fingers brushed over sensation packed nerve-endings in her tingling little clitoris, and Gerome knew that he was finally starting to get to her in a big way.

Enough of this horsing around, he instructed himself. Let's get down to some serious business! And he crawled purposefully back down over her milk-white body and began pushing her relaxed and unresisting thighs gently apart, his eyes trained on the hair-covered "vee" of her naked little pussy. The girl's lithe and lust inspiring form was now moving incessantly as his persistent pokes and prods aroused her more and more by the minute., and Gerome grinned as he wormed his lewdly prying fingers through the rounded cream-like spheres of her buttocks and tormented the soft red hair-lined lips of her unused, inexperienced young vagina.

Her mind still wandering in the drugged mists of semi-consciousness, and her eyes still lightly closed, Melanie was too stoned to wonder at the strangely powerful new emotions being provoked inside herself. All that she wanted now was to give herself body and soul to this mysterious, faceless, nameless figure who hovered over her, and she rejoiced as she felt his harsh sweating palms against the delicate softness of her inner thighs pushing her legs farther and farther apart and opening her up to him like a flower.

## CHAPTER THREE

The man's head descended slowly toward her gently trembling thighs and Melanie's body jerked convulsively as his lips invaded the privacy of her pubic mound. His hotly slavering tongue speared forward like a lizard in flight as the brutal molester planted a noisy wet kiss on the palpitating flanges of her slowly opening cunt.

"Ohhhhhh," she groaned piteously, and Gerome shot a worried look up over her heaving white breasts to her face, but the girl was still not conscious of precisely what was happening to her. Melanie's hands crept down to her high-set sensuous breasts and her fingers unconsciously continued to stroke the thickly swollen nipples, keeping them hard and erect while the big burly man burrowed in between her widely spread legs, his lips lapping away hungrily at the moist pink furrow of her loins as if he had completely lost his mind.

The criminally aroused girl began to thrash her head wildly from side to side, her hips jerking convulsively as his hotly searing tongue traced a lewd path up and down the full length of her narrow wet cuntal slit, occasionally forcing its depraved way into the elastic-rimmed opening of her palpitating little vagina. Then, farther down, the conscienceless man paused a moment to pay his lewd respects to the small circular opening of her pinkly clasping anus, bringing a special kind of agonized groan from her lips.

Gerome was amazed at the speed with which this strange young brunette was becoming excited. She was obviously not a girl with a great deal of experience in bed, in fact he could easily deduce from the tightness of her vagina, but she was becoming more erotically aroused by the moment and he realized that she was one of those women who are red-hot for sex without ever consciously realizing it. Once the marijuana had blunted the fine edge of her prudish morality, she became one hot little bitch and there were no two ways about it!

Nor had he ever expected to have a little fireball like this at his complete disposal. As he nosed his way through the sweet smelling little triangle of raven-black pussy hair for another merciless tongue-thrust up into the moist sanctuary of her defenseless vagina, he felt the orgiastic fluids from deep inside her lust-wracked body starting to flow and realized that she was enjoying this as much as he was, unconscious or not. And she was too excited and too doped up to fight off anything he did to her now. The sky was the limit as far as this chick was concerned!

Her hands snaked down into his thick, white-blond, hair, and Gerome felt the drugged young coed forcing his face even farther into the rapidly moistening mysteries of her freely flowing body as she groaned almost incessantly under the vicious tongue-lashing he was giving her. As he stuck his tongue directly into her tiny clasping pussy-hole, the man delightedly felt the smooth inner walls of her cunt contract with a definite sucking motion as if she wanted to seize it and drag it up inside of her. At the same time, the girl's long, finely tapered legs began to get into the act, slipping dexterously up around his neck and taking him prisoner as if she wanted to hold him there between her silk-soft thighs forever.

Every fiber in Melanie's body seemed to be burning with some slow all-consuming flame and each time the wildly sucking man tongue-fucked into her, the muscles in her thighs reacted and her hips thrust back up against his face. Her legs splayed apart even farther, instinctively giving him the greatest possible access to the most private part of her body, and Gerome played it for all it was worth. At last! He could not take another moment's delay. He had to have her, and now!

Breaking free of the deathgrip of her thighs, he slithered his eagerly tensed body up over hers, pausing only to bob his head down and nip teasingly at the flaccid yielding flesh around each turgid nipple until she groaned half-consciously for mercy. His long unsheathed dagger of make flesh moved in for the kill, and with one abrupt forward-flicker of his hips, he brought the fat, blood-engorged tip of his cock into immediate contact with the openly quivering lips of her well moistened cunt. Her thighs were spread as wide as humanly possible and the little wet furrow of her vagina seemed to be begging for it.

Gerome could hardly suppress an unfeeling snicker as he contemplated what the deceived young coed would think the following morning when she surveyed her ravaged body in the mirror and wondered what on earth could possibly have happened to her. He would love to be there to see it, and in fact, he could be, thanks to the concealed compartment and the two-way mirror.

Melanie's mind by this time was more fogged . and confused than ever. She had no idea what was happening to her and she only knew that there was a terrible longing emptiness at the base of her stomach, a void which screamed to be filled at any cost. Her firmly rounded buttocks were grinding back and forth as if a steady stream of electric current were passing through it, and Gerome had to struggle with her wildly contorting body just to hold her down on the bed. Then, suddenly reaching down between their tensely straining bodies with his hand, he guided the quivering shaft of his massively swollen cock directly into the target, running it up through the narrow valley of her buttocks and then posing it right at the eagerly seeping entrance to her vagina.

Melanie felt him push, testing the elastic-rimmed tightness of her warmly throbbing little vagina. The man was big and his bludgeoning rod of flesh was too thick for the narrow aperture. Gerome knew that he was going to have to fight his way in, but the sound-proofed walls of the room would prevent her screams from being heard on the street. Taking a deep breath and steadying himself on all fours, he shoved forward up between her trembling milk-white thighs.

"Nooooooh!" she screamed out as the man's lust-inflated cock forced its way past the tightly unwilling cuntal ring and buried its massive throbbing tip just inside the fragile fleshy walls of her cruelly stretched vagina. "Aaaaaaggghhh!!!"

But there was no turning back for Gerome now, and a little screaming did not bother him in the slightest. In fact, it increased his pleasure considerably and he shoved all the harder, deciding to finish the job of impaling her in one more quick lunge.

"Ugggh!" she gurgled in agony as he ploughed his way into her to the hilt, slamming up against her futilely writhing body until his balls slapped harshly against her unprotected little anus. The girl's long, splendidly-formed legs were once again moving wildly, knocking out frantically on either side of his hard pillaging body as she struggled uselessly to escape this ferocious assault. But it was hopeless and had she not been completely knocked out on marijuana, she would have seen precisely how hopeless it was. Each agonized jerk of her brutally implaced body only served to insert his hard-charging penis deeper into the warm moist softness of her cunt, and her piteous groans for mercy only stimulated the cruelly sadistic man to greater heights of depraved passion.

The drugged young coed's mind was thoroughly befuddled and she felt as if she were being split down the middle like a sacrificial lamb. The hard-skewering rod of flesh seemed to be running all the way up inside her body, so deep that she could almost taste it in the back of her throat. Her dazzled mind made a few tentative attempts to orient itself, but the clouds of marijuana prevented her from thinking clearly for as much as an instant. In her private dream world, the kindly protective Joe Brown had just changed back into her cruelly-smiling boyfriend Tony and she knew somehow that it would be a waste of time to beg him for mercy. He was punishing her for having cheated him that night in his father's car, and she deserved every bit of it.

Gerome looked down on the girl's nakedly suffering body with triumphant joy, knowing that she had never been penetrated at all. If she had been a virgin ten minutes ago, she was no longer a virgin now, and he had surged into her with such speed and determination that he had hardly noticed whether his bull-dozing cock had swept away the fragile membrane of her virginity or not. It did not make much difference now, and he smiled cruelly as he listened to the tormented howls of pain whimpering from her open mouth, and watched her arms outstretched on the pillow in total surrender as she writhed nakedly beneath him, her lips bared back over her teeth in a tight grimace of agony.

Trying to excite himself even more, the cruel whoremaster raised his great muscle-hardened body up in the air and gazed down to the point where his golden blonde pubic hair meshed lewdly with her faint dark fuzz, and his huge, lust-engorged cock disappeared up into the pinkly glistening flesh of her cunt. He held her still for a moment, enjoying the scene and savoring this moment of animal conquest, wishing there had been someone else there to see how skillfully he had dominated this sleek-bodied, heavy-breasted princess from another world.

Melanie was still thoroughly lost in her private universe of drug-ridden fantasy, but one thing was real and concrete to her; there was a man's long hard penis completely embedded in her formerly unpenetrated young vagina and she could feel every ridge and indentation in the long punishing rod. It wormed inside of her like some horrendous species of animal with its head nestled snugly against the delicate tip of her cervix and at the other end, she could feel the ridiculous tickle of his sperm-laden testicles as they danced lewdly in the narrow moist crevice of her buttocks. It had become a part of her now and somehow the pain seemed to be slowly receeding. She had wanted so desperately to be filled, filled at any cost, and now she was empty no longer!

The change in her body was slight, almost unnoticeable, but Gerome had been in a lot of beds in his time and the big man had grown sensitive to the moods of his sex-partners. Experimentally, he flexed his organ, bringing a soft whimper to her lips, but not the sullen cry of anguish he had expected.

It was working, he told himself triumphantly. The lust-stimulating marijuana had done the trick again. This little girl was already balancing precariously on the tightrope between agony and ecstasy!

He flexed his penis deep within her steaming cuntal flesh, withdrawing himself an inch or two and then worming his way back in to his original position. Her eyes remained tightly shut, but no sound of pain issued now from between her sensually parted lips. Yes, it was time for him to go to work!

Still moving slowly and cautiously, Gerome retreated until the heavy bulbous tip of his cock was left just inside her moist tender pussyhole and then ploughed smoothly forward, and the groan which involuntarily escaped from her lips told him clearly that she was no longer in any condition to object to anything he chose to do to her from now on. Her dark beautiful head was lolling from side to side on the soft whiteness of the pillow, and at the same moment, Gerome could feel the soft regular undulations of her hips as the rhythm of his strokes communicated itself to her love-starved body.

Despite the continuing fog in her brain, Melanie herself was partically conscious of the fact that her body was coming to life. The pain had departed now, replaced by a soft excruciating tingle which started somewhere deep down inside of her cock-stuffed belly and spread inexorably out through the rippling tissues of her cunt into the milk-white flesh of her widely-spread thighs. The strange, all-pervasive sensation worked its way up along her back bone until the unbearable stimulation arrived at the lewdly swaying twin peaks of her breasts, making her tiny brown nipples stand out even more strongly than before.

Gerome looked down upon her with unconcealed delight as he felt her hips begin to rotate lustfully from side to side and the tiny contracting muscles of her vagina start to nibble hungrily at the lust inflated head of his long stiffened penis. Every time the man surged brutally up into her, the widely-dilated lips of her hair-lined pink pussy slit seemed to cling to the blood filled thickness of his cock, disappearing up inside of her as he skewered forward. On the backstroke, the frail pink cuntal tissue seemed to cling to the thick blue-veined skin of his penis as if the girl was reluctant to let him go.

And her body movements were becoming fiercer and more frantic by the moment as her sexual tension increased. Her arms were wrapped tightly around his neck as if they had been lovers for a year, and the flat smooth plane of her stomach slapped into his slightly protuberant belly as she bucked beneath him like an untamed dilly. She was straining to cum, he realized, struggling like a madwoman for sexual release in the arms of a man she did not know and had never seen before!

Gerome found this bizarre situation extraordinarily stimulating and he grinned as he heard the lewd wet sluicing sound coming from between their two desperately straining bodies. Her knees were lifted high up off the bed now with the soles of her feet planted flat on the mattress and her head jammed cruelly up against the head-board of the bed. In her drug-dazzled mind, her lover had once again become the kind considerate young man she had met that day on the bus, and she cried to him with all her heart as the inexorable spasm began to sweep over her, tossing her tormented body like a ship swamped by a tidal wave.

"Ahhhhhh!!!" she sang to him. "Joe ... Joe ... it's happening to me! I'm cumming!"

Gerome nearly went out of his mind as she gurgled out this wildly erotic orgasm, running her sharp fingernails across the broad muscular expanse of his back and sucking voraciously on his tongue. The bouncer tried to hold back and prolong his own pleasure, but the pressure was too intensive for his incredibly excited cock to sustain. As her legs entwined around his lustfully pumping buttocks pulling him even farther up into the secret recesses of her womb, the white-hot heat and tension built up impossibly high in his wildly swinging crevice of her buttocks.

"You little whore!" he mumbled as the hot sticky cum poured irresistibly out of him. Melanie felt the head of his cock suddenly begin to swell and throb as if it were in the process of exploding, and then came the moment of release which both of them had instinctively been praying for. Like white-hot lava from an erupting volcano, his molten male cum stormed into her body, ricocheting around the grasping inner walls of her cunt as he creamed endlessly into her.

When the orgasm had finally ended, Gerome lifted himself up on both his arms, a foolish grin on his face, expecting to find her eyes open and looking at him with fear. Instead, she gave every indication of having gone to sleep. All the years of repressed sexual tension finally released, Melanie had succumbed finally to the pervasive effect of the marijuana she'd smoked and passed out cold.

"Sleep tight, little college girl," he told her unconscious form as he slowly removed his gradually deflating penis from her over-worked little cunt, "Because I got big plans for you tomorrow!"

* * *

Melanie awoke slowly like a patient coming out of the ether after an operation, becoming gradually conscious of her surroundings. Yes, it was the same room and somehow she saw that she had managed to fall asleep with the light still lit.

When she got her sleepy eyes all the way open, however, the real surprise awaited her. The glimsy shortie nightie she had worn to bed had somehow been ripped off her body and thrown on the floor! She had spent the entire night spread-eagled on the bed, naked as a baby and without so much as a sheet to protect her from the night air. Fortunately the room had been warm or she might have caught a serious chill.

Alarmed, Melanie pulled the covers up from the bottom of the bed and snuggled into the soft spacious mattress, noticing as she did so that portions of the sheet below her were stained for some reason. The whole situation perplexed her. As she moved, there was a dull ache between her legs, as if her period was beginning or she had just spent a particularly long afternoon on horseback. What did all of this mean?

Then she remembered the dream. What madness, yes, it all came back to her now, she had this hopelessly erotic dream about being in bed and making love to the boy named Joe whom she had met on the bus coming to Dallas. A shiver ran through her nakedly battered body as she trembled beneath the covers recalling that dream. The things she had permitted him to do to her! Naturally, since it had been a dream, all those perversely wicked things had come from deep within her own subconscious. There must be a streak of evil down deep inside of me, she decided, which only comes out while I'm sleeping!

Yes, it made sense. Melanie had had erotic dreams before, particularly after an evening in the back seat of Tony's father's car, although nothing as wild as this! They had always been fleeting, barely-remembered fragments, nothing as solid and realistic as this dream had been.

In fright, Melanie crossed her hands protectively across the two fearfully heaving mounds of her breasts, and gave a cry of unexpected pain. Her nipples were painfully bruised! One hand shot down between her legs and she produced another alarmed yelp. There were sensitive black-and-blue marks on the soft white skin of her thighs! And worse of all-she blushed even to think the thought-her maidenly little vagina felt as if MONGOL HOARDS had marched through it all night long! What did this mean?

One thing for sure, this had been no ordinary dream. From the looks of things, she could only guess that she had suffered some kind of sexual blackout which must also have involved ... she could hardly bring herself to admit it, but the evidence of her naked body was too clear to be denied ... since she had been alone in the room last night, she could only have done these things to herself. And it was time to stop using nice words for it. She had masturbated, masturbated wildly and there was no other explanation!

A feeling of bitter shame swept over the girl and she remembered all the vague lectures she had received from her mother about purity and wholesomeness. So this is what she had been talking about! Melanie tried to reassure herself by thinking logically that the depraved act had been involuntary and therefore not a sinful thing, but an intense feeling of guilt doggedly stayed with her and would not go away.

It must have been the bus ride, she decided. I got myself overtired and overexcited and then all that dirty talk about prostitutes with Joe....She suddenly realized that it had been Joe Brown's image she had embraced with such violent passion the previous night. God, how could she ever face him again?

Well, there was no point in spending the whole day morbidly dwelling on the dreadful thing which had happened to her. She had learned something profoundly frightening about herself, that was for sure, and she could think of no way of being positive that it would not happen again, but it was futile to sit around worrying about it hour after hour.

One thing was certain, however. It would be a good idea to get out of this hotel. Her room was clean and pleasant, but the total silence was already starting to get on her nerves. She noticed that she could hear nothing from the outside; no footsteps in the hall, or trucks passing or birds singing. It was nine o'clock in the morning and all around her there was the total silence of an undiscovered tomb. It was eerie and a little bit frightening.

There was something strange about Ruby's, she decided. For one thing, she had noticed in the taxi that the "hotel" was a long way from the university district, in a distinctly run-down section of the city. And the more she thought about Mr. Gerome, the manager, the less likely it seemed that troubled students would bring their problems to someone like him. She could not put her finger precisely on what it was that troubled her about the place, but she felt distinctly uneasy here and the sooner she checked in at the university, the happier she would be.

The first order of business was a hot bath. There was strange dried white stuff all over her legs and she plunged joyously into a tub of hot water and scrubbed until her body sparkled with cleanliness. Then she dressed quickly, re-packed and headed for the door.

The door was locked.

* * *

Ruby was sitting in an attractive stripped house-coat with her well-groomed greying black hair in curlers, her sweet grandmotherly face in a tight smile as she listened to her good friend Gerome recount his nocturnal adventures.

"So this proves what I been saying all along," he asserted.

"I'm still worried, Gerome dear, Suppose her father starts searching for her?"

"Look, we can sit her down and make her write two letters, one to the university saying that she ain't coming, and one to her parents telling him that she's already registered and havin' a ball. That way nobody worries."

"And you really think she'll bring the customers in?"

"Ruby, you been running a whorehouse for forty years now and you still don't know nuttin' about men," complained the bouncer eagerly. "First, this girl is the best looking piece of tail I seen in a dog's age, and anybody in their right mind'd give his eye teeth to stick their cock into her. On top of that, she's got real class. I mean she talks nice and acts like a real high class broad."

"And she doesn't want to have anything to do with an establishment like ours," pointed out Ruby, sipping a little dark rum from her habitual teacup.

"And that's just what makes it perfect. These guys are tired of the kind of broad who just flops on her back and spreads her knees. That little girl up-stairs is gonna fight like a wild cat and the John's will have to slap her around first if he wants to get any action out of her."

"So you think that this will stimulate our customers?"

"Wait a minute, you ain't heard the half of it," Proclaimed the sadistic whorehouse attendent. "This chick is real screwed up in the head because she really wants it worse than a bird wants worms. Once you get inside of her and start fuckin' around, she turns on like a clock radio. Man, you shoulda seen the sparks fly last night when I was riding her. What a wild cat she is!"

"Gerome, you're a knuckle-head, but you just may have something here," conceded the madam, starting to be convinced. "But what's her body like? No john is going to spend good money on some flat chested little college girl even if she can talk fancy and wiggle her hips."

"Ruby, you gotta see for yourself. Come on, we'll go and have a talk with the little lady and have an official inspection."

* * *

Melanie jumped as the door burst open without warning, but she recovered with surprising quickness and turned on her tormentors with real indignation.

"What's the meaning of this?" she stormed, knowing now that something underhanded was going on. "Why was that door locked?"

"See what I mean," said Gerome, turning to Ruby and behaving precisely as if she were not there. "A real hell-cat and she uses good grammar too."

"Yes, she's a nice-looking young lady as well. I didn't get a good look at her last night, but now I see what you mean. Are her tits real or is she wearing falsies?"

"Nah, that's all her," affirmed Gerome excitedly, stepping forward and adroitly squeezing one of Melanie's high full breasts before the girl had a chance to dodge away. "You, take off yer clothes and let Ruby get a good look at ya'."

"I'll do nothing of the kind...." Melanie began spiritedly, but the man's big hand came suddenly out of nowhere and caught her full on the side of the face, sending her sprawling across the bed.

"Do what I tells you, bitch!" he growled at her menacingly, but the gentle lady corrected her assistant sharply for this breech of good manners.

"No, Gerome, I really must ask that you cease that sort of thing at once. You know I do not tolerate violence in my presence."

"Ah, I'm sorry, Ruby. Would you like to step out of the room while I beat 'er up?"

"No, not in this case, because I think that this young lady will listen to reason. But in the future, if you find it necessary to use force, I would prefer that you employ that whip in the cabinet. The sting is quite adequate and, as you know, it leaves no marks. Our customers would not appreciate finding ugly bruises or black-and-blue marks on this charming young body."

"I insist. ,." Melanie began again, bewildered by all that was happening to her, but her eyes followed Gerome's movements as he obediently went to the cabinet on the wall, unlocked it, and extracted a cruel looking leather whip which he brandished in her face. Stunned, she fell silent and Ruby continued in her school teacher's voice.

"Now, as you see, young lady, we are in a position to give orders and expect obedience, so you will do what you are told. I would like to see you naked please."

"No!"

"Excellent," commented the madam. "She is very high spirited. The customers will certainly enjoy overcoming that kind of resistance. Gerome, please strike her moderately hard on the backs of her legs."

Melanie backed away in terror as the zealous goon moved forward, but he had her neatly trapped between the bed and the wall and there was no escape. With a sickening hiss, the whip sailed through the air and connected painfully with the soft flesh on the backs of her knees.

"Aaaggghhh!" she screamed hoarsely, trying to

.scramble over the bed while Gerome his her again as she struggled away from him, this time creasing the backs of her milk white thighs just below the twin half moons of her desirable young buttocks.

"Now, without further ado, kindly strip yourself naked," ordered the smiling greying lady, "or I shall step out of the room for a minute and allow Gerome to tear the clothes off of your body by brute force. I assure you he will use the whip very thoroughly if you put him to so much trouble."

Her cheeks smeared with tears, the girl realized that she had very little choice in the matter. Either she obeyed these two monsters or they would cut her to ribbons with that whip, and the intensely painful smarting on her legs informed her clearly that her courage had melted as far as the lash was concerned. Never in her entire life having known the slightest physical discomfort, she was discovering that she was not as brave as she thought she was. Gerome moved menacingly in her direction again, and her hands flew to the buttons on her blouse.

"Oh please...." she mumbled in fear and confusion. "Why?"

"Never mind the questions," snapped the brothel-keeper a little acidly. "You have twenty seconds to get naked or Gerome will use the whip again. You see how much he enjoys it."

There was no longer any question about complying with their demands. Frightened out of her mind, the tall lush dark haired young coed rapidly undid the buttons on her blouse and slid it off her smooth creamy shoulders. The short skirt dropped to the floor next, revealing her long tapered legs. Glancing at the pair nervously, Melanie fumbled with the snap on her brassiere and released the proud twin mounds of her full womanly breasts. Around her brown pointed nipples, the marks Gerome had left on her the night before were still visible and Ruby grinned sadistically at the sight. Melanie kept hoping they would say that they had seen enough and tell her to stop, but Gerome gestured with the whip at her frail white cotton panties and Melanie, blushing with shame and humiliation, bent from the waist and slipped them off, baring the battered and bruised region of her vagina to the cruel eyes which were trained upon her.

"Gerome, I believe this time you have found us a gold mine," commented Ruby, walking around the nakedly shivering girl and examining her from all angles with the critical eye of an expert. "She looks like a model from one of those men's magazines you've always got your nose in. She'll do very nicely."

"Wha ... what are you going to do with me?" quavered Melanie unhappily, finding her tongue at last.

Instead of snapping at her, Ruby smiled pleasantly for a change, patting one of the girls large, lust inciting breasts as she spoke.

"You, my dear, will be privileged to fulfill your true function as a woman," she explained with a kindly expression on her sweet old face. "Alas, I am too old and men no longer desire me. But you will drive them bananas!"

"My function ... I don't understand."

"These college girls ain't too bright," observed Gerome with scorn. "We gonna send some guys in here and you gotta fuck 'em. That clear enough for ya?"

It was. Her cheeks reddening into a deeper blush, Melanie's eyes burned with indignation.

"Never!" she spat back at them, finding her courage at last. "I would never do such a thing!"

"That's perfect," commented Ruby happily, glancing at her cohort. "See how her eyes flash."

"Yeah, she's gonna be great," agreed the whorehouse strongman. "We're gonna get rich with this little broad."

"I absolutely will not cooperate!" Melanie shouted, a little perplexed at their reactions. "I demand that you release me immediately or I will call the police."

To Melanie's utter consternation, this seemed to be precisely the way they wanted her to act, since the two brothel operators smiled at each other knowingly as Gerome began to gather up the girl's disgarded clothing and stuff it into her suitcase.

"Don't you understand?" she pleaded with them, totally confused by their attitude. "I'm not a prostitute. I ... I'm still a virgin!"

After all that had happened, Melanie was not totally sure that this was the strict scientific fact of the matter, but she calculated that they would hardly be in a position to dispute her. Unfortunately, her claim simply produced another round of rauchous laughter.

"Sure you are, baby," sneered Gerome. "Hey listen, did you have any strange dreams last night?"

At these words, the girl's mind really went into a tail spin. So it had not been her imagination! Something actually had happened the previous night!

"I ... I don't understand," she said, burying her face in her hands as she stood nakedly before them.

"Baby, you were great!" Gerome proclaimed crudely. "About the best fuck I ever had, and probably the best you've ever had too, although I'd like to know some more about this guy Joe you kept talking about."

Utterly demolished, the girl sank back on the bed, cowering beneath her two heartless tormentors while they poured a steady stream of harsh mocking laughter upon her.

"Didn't your mommy ever tell you about taking funny-looking cigarettes from strangers?" Gerome continued to rub it in. "Here's the rest of the pack, baby, you're gonna need 'em!"

## CHAPTER FOUR

It was nearly an hour before Melanie Abbott got ahold of herself and was able to think clearly. Walking naked around the small room, she tried her best to review the situation in her mind. Escape seemed to be impossible. The massive wooden door was locked securely from the outside and anyway Gerome had taken away her suitcase and all her clothing, leaving only her cosmetics case and the pack of marijuana cigarettes which were still lying at the foot of the bed.

Gradually, it all became clear to her. They were going to prostitute her! They were going to send men into this room, strange unknown men, who could do what they liked with her nakedly defenseless body.

A knock came at the door and the startled girl snatched up a blanket off the bed and covered herself as Gerome entered carrying a tray.

"You better get some breakfast, honey, because your work-day is about due to begin. First time in many a year that we've had customers in here before noon, but when we told 'em about you, the line started forming!"

Gerome still carried the whip stuck in his belt, but Melanie felt a little more self confident with the blanket wrapped around her and she made one last attempt to climb up on her high horse.

"Mr. Gerome," she began coolly. "I must inform you one last time that what you are proposing is quite impossible. I intend to defend my honor with all the strength in my body and each and every one of your so called customers will have a real fight on his hands if he tries to touch me. I realize that I can be beaten into some kind of submission, but surely that won't be much fun for your customers."

"That's what's gonna make it perfect, baby," the lewd brothel keeper replied with a satisfied smile. "The guys who are gonna come walking in here like nuttin' better than a little fight before they do their stuff. It kinda gets 'em excited, understand? Everybody's tired of the kinda broad who just lays there and spreads her legs. You fight all you want, honey, and old Gerome will get rich!"

With this unfeeling pronouncement, he laid the tray at the foot of the bed and left, carefully relocking the door behind him. Melanie sat down in a daze, now having a whole new set of facts to consider. So they wanted her to resist! It was part of their plan that she should go down fighting!

There were waffles, bacon and rich black coffee on the tray and Melanie wisely decided that she should take at least this much advice from Gerome and eat a hearty breakfast. God only knew what kind of horrors were going to come walking through that door in a matter of minutes and she could defend herself better on a full stomach.

She thought as she munched on the waffles, trying to consider every aspect of the problem. Gerome was obviously a man who likes girls better if they had to be taken by force, and it was only logical to assume that there must be many other men like him in the world. Strange that her parents had never mentioned this kind of thing, but then the young girl was starting to discover that there were quite a few unpleasant facts in this world which her mother and father had neglected to explain.

So what was the best strategy for resistance? Even without the whip, Gerome could easily overpower her any time he wished, and she had to assume that the kind of man who liked to bully girls would not be the ninty-seven pound weakling type. Probably they would all be able to beat her into obedience quite easily and putting up a battle with each one of them would only mean more fun for them and more pain for her. Somehow she had to ruin their pleasure so they would let her go. But how?

The answer was ridiculously simple. She must not resist, not in the slightest.

She must lie there utterly passive, and spoil their depraved lewd enjoyment.

But somehow, she sensed in the back of her head that she would never be able to do it that way. Even wanting to put up no resistance, she realized that the rigid moral training she had received as a child was far too strong. She would fight back whether she wanted to or not. And the customers would cheerfully beat her black and blue, fling her fomented naked body around on this very bed and ravish her with even greater delight. She would be playing into their hands one way or another. If she only had sleeping pills or something to knock herself out with! If she could only avoid being conscious when it happened!

Melanie finished her breakfast and drained the cup of coffee, surprised that her appetite was as good as it was, considering the terrible situation she was in. Settling back on the bed to do some more thinking, she found herself vaguely wishing for a cigarette. She could have asked Gerome to....

Suddenly, her glance fell on the doped cigarettes he had scornfully left for her and she remembered what the marijuana had done to her poor dazzled mind the night before. Of course, smoking dope was a very wicked thing to do, something only moral degenerates indulged in, but in a situation like this, one had to chose the least of all available evils. If she smoked enough to dull her brain, to deaden her sensibilities-it had worked last night!

\* \* \*

Melanie puffed furiously on the cigarette, trying desperately to draw the strong harsh smoke down into her lungs where it would give her the maximum effect. Her legs tucked under her and covered with a blanket, the girl's ripely swelling breasts were quivering with real terror as she struggled to drug away her consciousness before her first "visitor" presented himself. Her mind was wracked with images of the terrible things which she understood were going to happen to her. Strange dirty men who like to torture women would come and lay their hard hands upon her nakedly defenseless body, skewering into her heartlessly and brutally, unmindful of her screams for mercy.

She had to get high! Sucking furiously on the cigarette and longing for the deadening sensation of the marijuana, she lit a second cigarette before the first was quite finished, and had just inhaled as deeply as she could when the door slid silently open.

Oh God, I'm not out yet, she groaned to herself. I'm still wide awake! Why isn't this stuff working?

"Okay, and if you find she's more than you can handle, don't hesitate to use the whip," Gerome was telling her first customer as he stepped into the room. "But try not to mark her too badly. We've got a whole string of other clients to think about and she has to be kept in reasonably good shape for awhile at least."

"Okay, Chief," commented a short stout muscular man as he followed Gerome into the room. "I won't damage the merchandise. Hot damn! She looks like she might be worth that outrageous price you're asking. See y'later."

Gerome grunted and disappeared, locking the door securely behind him while the newcomer walked slowly toward the bed, unbuttoning his shirt as he came, his dark malicious eyes gleaming with anticipated pleasure. Melanie watched him approach, sucking wildly on the cigarette and wondering what she should do. Perhaps she could somehow confide in this man, explain the situation and convince him to help her escape. It seemed un-likely, but at this point, anything was worth a try.

"Sir, if you could listen to me a moment," she began hesitantly, but she fell immediately silent as he sadistically waved the whip in her face.

"Don't like chatty dames," he informed her brutally. "Shut yer trap and spread yer legs."

Melanie cowered under the blanket while the man placidly continued undressing and she failed to repress a gasp as he lowered a soiled pair of undershorts, revealing a heavy fat belly and beneath that, a short thick cock which dangled limply between his hairy thighs. He approached the bed and violently yanked the blanket away from her and the terrorized girl took one last drag on the cigarette before it was knocked out of her hand and the man was on top of her.

Pinning her roughly to the bed, his hard calloused hands roamed lustfully over her struggling naked body, squeezing her tiny brown nipples until they hardened involuntarily beneath his fingers and digging with the other hand into the light soft pubic hair between her fearfully convulsing legs. Melanie struggled futilely, trying to push his hard musclar arms away and wiggle off the bed, but he was easily twenty times too strong for her and laughed harshly at her ridiculous attempts to escape. His huge fat chest shaking with laughter, he played with her like a child plays with a helpless kitten, turning her this way and that and examining her splendidly vulnerable body from all angles.

Suddenly Melanie let herself go completely limp and in this moment of relaxation, the frail bodied young woman discovered that the marijuana had worked after all, but not quite the way she had expected. Instead of putting her to sleep, the drug was electrifying every fiber in her body and each time this rough unfeeling man touched her, he set off a whole chain reaction of tiny pleasurable sensations which raced through her abused flesh like a thousand miniature needles.

Instead of drifting peacefully off to sleep, she was turning on more violently every minute! Her body felt like a forest of dry trees with a fire raging wildly out of control, her mind gallantly fighting a hopelessly losing battle for survival. Melanie lay immobile for a few minutes, taking deep breaths and trying to regain control over her own drug weakened flesh, but moaning as the cooling air swept over the exposed little button of her clitoris. The muscles in her smoothly molded thighs flexed and unflexed convulsively and the high proud peaks of her breasts rose and fell rapidly with every panting breath.

The man was enjoying himself enormously, perfectly unaware of the raging mental conflict going on inside the young girl's tortured head. That obscene man, Gerome, had told him that this was a kidnapped college coed who was being held here against her will, but he was not about to swallow a story like that. She was a whore, just like any other whore, but after all, it was really the act which counted and this gal was putting on a performance worthy of an acting award. He had never seen a woman turn on so quickly and so violently in his life, but it made not the slightest difference to him if she enjoyed herself or merely pretended to enjoy him. He was having a ball, and that was all that counted!

And he decided then not to wait a moment longer to experience the real thing. Pushing her unresisting thighs farther apart with the calloused palms of his hands, he levered up over her like an avenging angel, his short broad cock dangling between his legs like a sword ready for action. The bed sagged as the cruel visitor crawled into position up between her wide spread legs and Melanie began to feel within herself that same irrational hungering emptiness she had known the night before. There was an enormous need throbbing down between her widely spread thighs, a space which was now suddenly screaming to be filled at any cost.

Gerome and Ruby were gone and forgotten now. What she needed was a cock, a man's big cock and she needed it badly. Her mind was repelled and horrified by the man's fat corpulent body but he was all that was available and he would have to do. Panting with a sudden desperate lust, she arched her hips up to meet him, spreading her legs out obscenely on either side of her just waiting for him. The visitor, needed no further invitation, he unexpectedly released his arms and allowed his heavy body to crush down onto hers, knocking all the wind out of her and flicked his hips forward at the same time in an effort to penetrate her in one quick movement. He missed, his fat stubby penis stabbing unseeingly between the entrancingly undulating half moons of her buttocks, challenging the unprotected nether entrance of her little anus. But this was not what he wanted and while she groaned in angry frustration, he reached down below his stomach and used his fingers to guide the throbbing blood engorged head of his cock directly into her hotly waiting cunt, worming into her as far as he could go with one powerful thrust. His obscenely swaying balls slammed lewdly against the helplessly upthrust surface of her ass and the man groaned with satisfaction as he sank into her as far as he could go.

But it was not far enough for Melanie! Thinking he was not yet all the way in her, the drugged girl wiggled her hips wildly trying to force him deeper into her half empty hungering cunt. Then she sobbed with the horrid realization that he had already given her all the cock he had to offer.

"O ... please ... go deeper," she urged him, a hot furious flame spreading quickly over her cheeks as she listened to herself utter these shamefully obscene words, hardly able to believe that this was she, Melanie Abbott, the well raised and proper young coed who had spoken them. Yet it was all true! A sense of wild frustration and intense disappointment was spreading rapidly through her over stimulated body. She had prepared herself emotionally and physically to be cruelly raped,, penetrated and abused and she unconsciously believed that this man would be able to do with her body what Gerome had done the night before. Without realizing it she had been looking forward to having pleasure forced upon her!

And now that pleasure was being denied and the full breasted, voluptuous young brunette found herself groaning piteously with a strange warped combination of unfulfilled lust and bitter, humiliating shame.

But her first customer was defintely trying to do his best. Worming his tongue expertly into her open panting mouth, he tired to make up for his frustrating lack of a satisflying cock with a surplus of energy. Pistoning his short blood filled cock into her nakedly writhing body with all the lustful strength in his thick heavy body and it did help a little. Melanie felt her body grow warm again as she labored frantically under him, her mind still spinning like a buzz-saw from the effects of the marijuana. A few more minutes, she was telling herself in her drug induced state, if he can keep it up for another few minutes....

But he could not, unfortunately, and the young girl felt his inadequate cock stiffen suddenly within her hot clasping cuntal depths, and listened as the man let out a long, soul strickened moan of pure pleasure, sighing while the white hot liquid sperm flowed copiously into the tortured recesses of her frantically clasping little cunt.

Melanie's body churned wildly in a last ditch effort to cum too, but the effort was destined to be in vain. She had been only inches away from ecstasy, but that inch was as good as a mile and she sobbed in frustration as she felt the man's useless flaccid cock slowly deflate and slip out of her still unsatisfied vagina. The customer was perfectly aware that he had failed her, but the situation did not bother him much at all. Gerome had tried to convince him that this gal was a prisoner of some kind, but as far as he was concerned she was just another whore. Sure, a good deal better looking than most, but still a whore at heart. Whether or not she enjoyed herself in bed with him was a matter of complete indifference as far as he was concerned. She was just lucky that he had not used the whip on her this time!

He smiled at her sadistically as he climbed briskly into his pants, but the unusual new prostitute had closed her eyes tightly and had rolled over on her side, her nakedly splendid body now quivering with heart-breaking sobs. Whatever her problem was, it was not his, and the heavy man whistled contendly as he walked out the door.

The marijuana was really starting to hit her now and Melanie could feel her head spinning insanely despite her persistent attempts to decide what to do next. She knew that she ought to be planning her escape or trying to figure out some way out of this horrible slavery, but somehow the canabis swamped brain cells in her head refused to function properly and her mind was alive with weird erotic thoughts and fantasies. Horrible depraved dreams she could not control! The room was comfortably warm, but her naked body was shivering with an unsatisfied burning lust which she could not forget or ignore, no matter how hard she tried.

The sexual hunger was driving her mad, and with a shock at her obscene thought, Melanie realized that she desperately wanted another man! Anyone at all would do, just so long as he were male and able to do the job she needed done. Hurry, she pleaded inside her drugged brain. Don't make me wait like this!

"Don't take the whole day there, 'Doc'," Gerome was saying to someone at the door, "'cause there's a big line down there and they ain't got all day. If she gives you too hard a time, bang on the door and we'll send up a couple of guys to sit on her while you do your stuff. And here's the whip. It might come in handy."

"If you'd be so kind as to disappear, my good man," replied Melanie's next customer. "I'm quite capable of managing this kind of thing for myself, thank you!"

The newcomer was well into his sixties and he looked as if he might really be a doctor of some kind, and for a moment, Melanie was caught in a confused moment of indecision. From the sound of his voice when he dismissed Gerome, he had seemed like well educated, established person, the type who could be reasoned with, even if he had lowered himself to a visit to a place like this. On the other hand, her slender young body was still burning with that same all consuming flame of lust, and yielding to the terrible temptation, she decided to let him satisfy her first, and if she succeeded in pleasing him too, he might then be well disposed towards helping her escape from here.

Melanie tried to speak, but for some reason no words came out so she simply lay doubled up with her knees drawn up against the fully curving mounds of her high young breasts with her hands covering her face as the old man slowly approached the bed. He was wasting no time, however, and by the time he had reached her, he was as naked as she. The white curly hair on his chest contrasting sharply with the youthful muscle tone of his body and he was in good shape for his age. His long shriveled cock dangled obscenely down between his legs and it was getting harder and firmer with every passing second.

The old man was beside himself with delight. Normally, he had to content himself with the tried fat whores he could find on the street, but it had been years or even decades since he had had a woman this young and succulent to play around with. Without any further ceremony, he climbed quickly up on the bed, throwing one leg over her so that he straddled her stomach, looking down into her drugged, lust contorted face with the gleaming eyes of a maniac.

Like himself, his cock was aging and was well past the age of retirement.

But the old timer had managed to keep both of them fairly active in recent years, and the ancient instrument sprang into life as his bony hands rudely caressed her fully ripened breasts.

The deadly narcotic in Melanie's dazed head made the room seem to whirl like a merry-go-round and she flopped on her back and gripped the edges of the mattress tightly with her hands as if she were in danger of sliding off onto the floor. What was he waiting for, she cried to herself, shivering with fear and anticipation, and desperately wanting even this ancient cock to come skewering into her aching belly and fill that awful void inside of her for once and for all with his rigidly throbbing cock. But the man seemed unusually preoccupied with her pink pointed nipples, as he inched farther and farther up on her sensually squirming torso until his long wrinkled penis lay in the delicate valley between her two soft breasts, using his hands to tweak and twist her tiny hard nipples until she thought she was going to go clear out of her mind.

The girl was horribly confused, but the elderly client knew precisely what he wanted of this voluptuous, young beauty and he put one hand on each of her heavy sensuous breasts and pushed them firmly together and in doing so trapped his lustfully jerking cock in between them.

"Oh please...." she begged, too far under the influence of the marijuana even to feel some shame for what she was saying. "Not like that. Do it the regular way, please!"

If he heard what she was saying, the aging man gave no sign of it and his lustful grin simply grew wider as he began to rock back and forth on top of her, sliding his long blue veined cock in and out of the narrow valley he had artifically created with the soft flesh of her trembling breasts.

"No ... no ... do it to me!" she pleaded, thrashing her head back and forth as she tried desperately to clear her marijuana fogged brain. The old man ignored her, thrusting his lust enlarged cock frantically back and forth between her tightly pressed breasts. Despite her confused condition, Melanie could feel the smooth bulbous tip of his penis growing larger and more firm as it pummeled the delicate white skin of her breasts, appearing high on her chest and then disappearing again like a snake scuttling back into its hole.

The "Doc" was panting with exertion, but there was no question of his giving up now. He was almost ready to cum and Melanie gasped and turned her head with horror as she felt her nakedly vulnerable breast and neck being sprayed with the hot sticky cum from his aged rod. The thick viscous sperm flowed over her soft white shoulders and down onto the sheet, and the old man left her as quickly as he had come. The next thing she knew, he was quietly putting on his shoes at the foot of the bed, whistling cheerfully to himself.

"Please, I'm being held a prisoner here," Melanie managed to stammer, pulling the blanket up over her naked cum drenched breasts. "Can you help me? Oh please, help me? Just call the police for me."

If the old man even heard her, he gave no indication of it and adjusted his clothing in the mirror one last time before rapping on the door with his cane to be let out. It was hopeless! None of these people were ever going to help her. If they went to the police on her behalf, they would only be exposing themselves to the possibility of arrest.

The tormented young coed groaned in agony, realizing that she was getting nowhere, and for a moment she felt like weeping with despair. There was only one way out of this misery and as soon as he disappeared out of the door, she lunged for the pack of drugged cigarettes on the table beside the bed. If she could smoke her way into oblivion, then the matter would be out of her hands. At the moment she was still rational enough to think clearly and as long as she could, she would understand what was happening to her and feel shamed and degraded as a result. Her lust ridden body was going to betray her again anyway, that much was certain, but it would all be much easier if she didn't know what was going on around her.

She managed to light another cigarette, her hands shaking badly, just before Gerome marched into the room accompanied by a half dozen other grinning men.

"Enjoy your little cigarette break, honey," he smiled at her with false kindness, "because now your work is really going to begin."

"Wha ... what are you going to do?" she quavered seizing that opportunity to drag as deeply as possible on the drugged cigarette, to bombardin her lungs with the mind killing, lust inciting narcotic smoke.

"Just another customer," Gerome shrugged, winkinng at the other men in the room. "But this one is a little bit special and so I brought the boys in to enjoy the show."

"Oh, no, I can't," she whimpered. "Not with everyone watching me. Please

1

don't make it worse than it already is."

"Now, now," Gerome smiled with mock sympathy. "A gal with all you have to offer shouldn't be ashamed to let these fine gentlemen see what they've paid good money for. Besides, you're going to get to know them all very, very well before the afternoon is over, so there's no reason to get shy on us now, is there, honey."

Melanie tried her best to ignore them all and concentrate on the central task of knocking herself out completely. If she could somehow become unconscious, they coould do what they liked with her tormented body and it would be nothing more than a bad dream when she awoke. They could even hurt her if they wanted to, because the pain was no longer important. What she had to avoid was the disgrace and humiliation of being ravaged in the middle of a crowded roomful of lusting depraved men. God only knew what they had lined up for her to do now!

But unfortunately, the marijuana was only doing half of the job. Instead of rendering her unconscious, it was merely exciting her sexual appetite to an uncontrollable level. She was playing their game perfectly, whether she knew it or not!

"Come on in, Tommy," Gerome was calling to someone in the hall. Melanie tried to cover her nakedness with the cum soaked sheet and got one last desperate puff on the oigarette before she caught sight of a huge shadowy figure stooping to get through the doorway. The tortured, doped girl looked up in horror to meet her next lover and her eyes widened with sudden desperate fear.

He was the largest man she had ever seen, at least seven feet tall with a thick ponderous body. His face seemed pleasant and open, but from the good natured teasing manner the other men treated him, it was clear that this man was not as bright as he might be. All of his strength was in his massive muscular body with nothing left over for his brain, and Melanie saw pure dumb lust come into his blank eyes as he surveyed her poorly covered body. The other men in the room sent up a chorus of bawdy laughter and fell to work undressing the dumb giant, stripping him in a matter of seconds and then stepping back to admire his fantastic figure.

Melanie looked too, much as she wanted to shut her eyes and die right there on the spot. Tommy was already sexually aroused and his rigidly bobbing cock stuck out stiffly in front of him, grotesquely long and menacing. It looked to the frightened trembling girl on the bed to be the size of a baseball bat and the thick bulbous head of his huge cock seemed to be at least two inches in diameter.

It's a vision, Melanie found herself thinking in an agony of fear. This is something the marijuana is doing to me, it can't be true! He's too big! He'll kill me!

But Tommy stepped cheerfully up to the bed, an untroubled smile on his idiot's face as the crowd of men clustered around him, all anxious to see this incredibly lurid spectacle. Melanie slowly inched away from the monster as he approached her and she heard Gerome's voice issuing a terse order.

"Get her, boys! Hold her down!"

Instantly, the terrorized young brunette felt herself surrounded-by the men and their hard demanding hands seized her arms and legs and pulled her spread eagled onto her back. Her fragile pink pussy slit was quickly exposed to the full view of every one of the men in the room and the group feasted their lewd gaze on the moistly palpitating tangle of curls between her struggling legs. A few of the men got ahead of the game, stealing a quick pinch of her full exposed breasts or stroking the soft inner flesh of her lurching thighs as they pinned her helpless figure to the mattress of the bed.

Melanie's normally attractive face was contorted with panic as the feeble minded giant climbed onto the bed between her widely spread thighs, he looked down at her like a starving man gazes at a feast. The whole flat plane of Melanie's naked pussy was open and vulnerable to him, offered up to his lusts like some weird indian sacrifice, and the man grinned idiotically at her, stroking his immensely thickened cock with his hands to bring the powerful organ up to its full state of hardness.

The agonized young girl found it impossible to close her eyes and fade off into the unconsciousness she had worked so hard to attain Instead, her horrified gaze was locked on the man's lewdly swaying penis that was looming menacingly a few short inches from the soft moist crevice of her womanhood.

"Give it a little lick, big boy," suggested a few ol the voices from the room.

"Yeah, let's see that tongue of yours go to work," agreed another chorus excitedly.

He obeyed instantly, Tommy was apparently more interested in putting on a good show for his friends than in appeasing his own powerful desires. With an abrupt motion of his hairy body, his head dropped quickly between her finely tapered thighs, his lips closing over the delicate sensitive flesh between her legs. Slowly and torturuosly, his tongue began to explore the mysteries of her wide spread loins, lashing mercilessly over the young soft lips of her slowly clasping vagina and teasing the tiny pink tip of her clitoris until he forced a groan of pure agony from the girls open mouth.

Not yet satisfied, he jammed two fingers into her already battered cunt, cruelly spreading the fluttering hair covered lips of her vagina before removing them and returning again to the attack with his tongue. Melanie gritted her teeth, trying in vain to will away the overwhelming storm of forbidden sensations which were shooting wildly around her helplessly tortured body. Once again, her sensual nature was about to betray her and she could feel it coming a long way off, no matter what she tried to do to hold herself in control.

The giant's tongue was rapidly reducing her to a ' quivering mass of trembling burning flesh, and the marijuana she had smoked earlier was helping him and not helping her at all! As his lips licked furiously over the defenseless cuntal flesh around her tiny little vaginal hole, the same hungering desire came floating back over her. His tongue was just not going to do the job alone, and she wanted the real thing inside of her, a cock! No matter how much she struggled against the lewd erotic thoughts which pounded through her drugged brain, she knew with absolute conviction that she was sliding off into the brink of lust again.

She tried with all of her strength to hold on to her sanity, but the sexually arousing tongue fucking she was getting at the hands of this stupid man was too intense. Acting without instructions from her fogged brain, the girl's mouth suddenly began to babble.

"Oooh ... please ... fuck up inside of me," she groaned, starting to use the words she had heard Gerome say. "Yes, fuck me! Fuck me with your cock!"

The idiotic giant was accustomed to obeying orders and it was difficult to imagine a command more inviting than that one. Grinning, he lifted his lips from the sweet tasting moisture of her pussy and crawled remorselessly forward over her writhing body, pausing momentarily to bite the high pointed mounds of her breasts as he worked his way up the length of her naked squirming body. Meanwhile, Melanie hips were gyrating wildly in a frantic search for the huge pole which she knew in her heart was too large for her frail and inexperienced young body to accept. He was going to rip her to shreds, she knew, and somehow in her drug induced insanity, she wanted the pain and the torment, irrationally believing that she deserved to be punished for her sins.

The punishment was not long in coming! With an evil flick of his hips, the huge man skewered the blood filled tip of his cock forward, searching for her small cuntal opening and he found it almost immediately. He angled for position, feeling the heavy murderous tip of his rod penetrating past the pinkly moistening lips of her vagina and gliding into her until it encountered the fragile elastic ring of her cuntal opening. He pushed, trying to break past the resisting barrier, and flashes of pain shot through her over wrought body. She screamed, flinging her head wildly to one side in anguish.

"Aaaggghhh!!!" she whimpered.

But she was destined to be ignored. This was precisely why Ruby had gone to the trouble of having sound proofing put in the room and so there was no danger that the girl's agonized screams could be heard on the streeet where they might catch someone's attention.

The half wit, Tommy, was in no mood to wait until she had recovered and he thrust eagerly forward again, forcing the thick broad tip of his huge cock another few inches up into her vainly resisting cuntal passage. Melanie screamed again, louder this time, and the harsh restraining hands holding her body pressed harder to hold her down fast to the bed as she bucked and struggled to escape.

How she regretted her reckless desire of a few minutes before to be punished for her sins! Now she was being punished good and proper and it was more than she could handle. She realized that his penis was too large and that she could never accept all of it into her tender vaginal opening. She would be split apart and she would be destroyed for life ... assuming she lived through the horrible, experience at all!

But Tommy hardly cared what was happening to her. In his weak mind, he was only aware that he had never in his life felt anything as soft and moist as this pretty girl's cunt he was stabbing into and the sooner he was all of the way in, the happier he would be. He pushed again and again, inching his torturous way forward up between the tight straining of her legs, and ignoring her impassioned pleas for mercy, while the cruel motley crowd of men who surrounded her bed carefully watched her face just waiting for the first signs of acceptance or at least surrender.

Melanie was only dimly aware of their presence, only half feeling their lewd hands pawing at her breast and buttocks and barely hearing them make rude comments to one another as they watched this obscene spectacle unfolding before them.

"Come on, Tommy," she heard Gerome urging. "You got another two inches more to go, boy. Hurry up, 'cause we ain't got all day."

Before these words could register on the girl's drug hazed brain, the subnormal youth obeyed, using all the power in his enormous haunches to slam brutally forward, his cock pushing tiny ripples of stubbornly resistant cuntal flesh along with it as he rolled into her with one strong movement, burying the remaining two inches of his long thick cock into the softly accepting moistness of her violated young cunt.

Melanie's body almost flew off the bed as his heavily swinging balls crashed moistly into the unprotected cheeks of her buttocks and she felt as though a giant boa constrictor had crawled up inside of her, crushing all the internal organs of her body and filling her so that she could barely breathe.

His penis seemed to fill her all the way up to the back of her throat, and for a few minutes the sensation was neither pain nor pleasure but a combination of both, so intense that she could hardly decide which was greater.

Despite his limited intelligence, Tommy held still for a moment, allowing the helplessly pinned girl to adjust to the presence of his enormous penis in her helplessly skewered belly. The room was silent with anticipation and all eyes were on her. If she passed out now, their fun would be ruined. Gently, Tommy flexed his penis, bringing a low moan to her parted lips, but when he flexed a second time, she merely whimpered, showing that the cruelly stretched flesh of her filled cunt was gradually adjusting to this massive invasion.

There were expressions of amazement in the room as the group of aroused, lusty men remarked obscenely on the fantastic stretching ability of the female sexual organ. No one had really believed that Tommy would have been able to penetrate that tiny, almost virginal opening, but he had and the girl was still in one piece. Slowly, the big man began to revolve his hips, trying to increase the suffering aperture enough to give him some room to move around, and Melanie groaned in discomfort as she felt the strained muscles in her cunt being called upon to expand even more.

Meanwhile, the men in the tiny room were quickly going out of their minds with lustful anticipation. Gerome kept slapping at them and shouting for them to stop fondling Melanie, but they were quickly getting out of control, Melanie's heaving body was now tormented from a dozen different directions at once. One man was crouched in between Tommy's legs putting his hand underneath her ass to attackk the tiny nether ring of her anus, testing the strength of the tiny little hole with his probing middle finger. Another man had fastened his mouth around the soft yielding flesh of her left breast and was sucking madly on her throbbing nipple. But Tommy ignored them all, he was concentrating on the job immediately at hand, his hips already beginning to fall into a slow in and out fucking motion.

The pain was fading away gradually and Melanie felt an insane feeling of happiness flooding through her drug dimmed body. She could not really think in the usual sense of the word and she was reduced to animal feelings by being unhappy while something was hurting her, aand joyful when something gave her pleasure and it was as simple as that! Moral issues no longer counted, just the feelings of basic animal lust and pleasure ... that was all that mattered to her now. Her mind was slowly dropping to a lower level of consciousness and her hips reacted by gyrating in tiny little circles in an obscene rhythm goaded by the probings of Tommy's pumping, hard cock.

"Yes, yes, yes," she began to chant mindlessly. "Fuck me like that...." With the dozen lewd hands all obscenely mauling her body, she squirmed in a new found sensuality as the men around her excited themselves into an insane frenzy of sexual excitement.

"Don't stop! Don't stop! That's right, just like that!" she pleaded, her educated accent sounding a little ridiculous in this depraved situation. But at last she was on her way to cumming, and her jubilant body heaved and spun as her hunger grew more intense and insatiable by the moment. She was building inexorably toward her climax, a powerful orgasm which no one could take away from her. In another minute, in another few strokes, and she would make it at last. Freed from the gnawing merciless need she had been feeling deep down in the freely flowing depths of her belly. She snaked her hands down to the man's buttocks, urging him to pound into her cunt harder and faster, but unexpectedly the brute began to slip and the wild fear ran through her mind that she would be cheated again.

"No, please, don't stop!" she begged, but the moment was already upon them and nothing could stop it now. Tommy's moranic eyes rolled back in his head and his huge sperm ladened testicles began to discharge their white milky cum into the yearning cuntal recesses of her starved young body. Her nakedly wide split cunt ground desperately into him with fantastic urgency, but he was holding still now, and his cock was spewing endlessly into her with every muscle in his long massive body. Her movements only hastened the end for him and not for her, and his penis was already becoming soft and useless and the oversized man then rolled off of her with a satisfied sigh. He was completely drained. After three customers, she was virtually bathed in cum, but no closer to the heights she was craving for with all her heart and soul.

There was no time for reflection now, even if her narcotic filled mind had been capable of thinking rational thoughts. All hell was goiing on around her and the room was filled with Gerome's harsh shouts as he tried to re-establish order among the excited crowd of eager men. All hoping to be next in line, most of them had stripped away their clothing and several men had climbed on the bed simultaneously and were wrestling with one another in their haste to fuck into her willing, well moistened cunt. There were men's bodies all over her and Melanie closed her eyes and gave up trying to keep track of them all, not particularly caring anymore who won the contest, so long as someone came shooting into her belly as soon as possible.

It was cock she wanted, nothing more. The cock did not need a face or a personality attached to it, so long as it was hard and straight and thickly swollen and capable of doing the job she wanted done. One man seemed to have fought his way into the saddle and the girl raised her hips to receive him like a blessing. She never did manage to distinguish his face, but his thick long penis was excited and hard and he drove right into her pussy without a moment's foreplay or preparation.

He had no sooner started when the long denied release hit her with the full force of a tidal wave breaking across the beach and sweeping everything away with it. Joy, pure, solid, and unmistakable, flooded over her as the man began to spew endlessly into her, adding his own little offering of cum to the flood which had already been left there by the others in that long lewd morning. As the orgasm swept over her passionate body, she wallowed gloriously in a sea of cum and a thousand cocks and for awhile, the no longer innocent young girl floated off into her own private dream world, losing track of the confusion going on all around her in the room.

When she finally became more conscious again, she had been rolled over on to her stomach, her legs stretched unnaturally far apart, and a different man was shooting off from behind up into her cum soaked, totally happy little cunt. Gerome was shouting directions, acting like a coach as the men crawled over her battered and abused body like a swarm of bees. She was conscious enough to enjoy the man behind her, even though she could not see his face, but she could feel the heavy, blunt end of his penis stuck rudely in the dripping wet crevice of her cunt. He slammed forward pushing her roughly up a few inches on the bed until her face was at the edge of the mattress. Then the dazzled young brunette felt another pair of hands seize her head in a savage death grip and turn her face towards him. The man was standing next to the bed with his rigidly erected cock thrust crudely in the girl's face and lying along side of her cheek.

Even when perfectly normal, Melanie would not have understood precisely what he was up to, and in her dazed state, she was totally perplexed, since the man seemed to be rubbing the broad seeping head of his penis across the trembling delicate surface of her full lips. This struck her as a strange thing and she opened her mouth to utter a protest. It was a fatal move. With lightening speed, the unknown man shoved forward, thrusting his fully erect member into the wet dark sanctuary of her mouth before she could get her wits together and snap her teeth defensively shut.

She was impaled at both ends now and the man in front of her began to saw furiously in and out of her mouth as if it were simply another cunt for him to violate as he wished. Melanie gagged at the pulsating hugeness in her throat, as the man sank his cock up into her unwilling mouth almost to the hilt and his balls slapped obscenely against her delicate skin with every blood thirsty plunge. Struggling to breathe, Melanie had no time to adjust to his depraved new invasion since another man then seized one outstretched hand and fastened her fingers tightly around his cock whhile someone else was tormenting the firmly rounded moons of her buttocks. She was surrounded by men, all doing their best at once to use her nakedly defenseless body for their own peculiar pleasures.

It was a real orgy, but Melanie had ceased to care very much at this point about the indignities being heaped upon her vulnerable young body. In fact, it was the very helplessness of her position which was beginning to excite her powerfully. She was being fucked brutally back and forth between two total strangers whose faces she had never seen and whose names she did not know, and the whole idea began to excite her even more. For some reason, perverse or not, she wanted to be used like this, and the more brutal, the better!

Slowly, the tall brunette began to react again, her buttocks undulating backwards with increasing speed while she experimented with the penis that was in her mouth. Normally, the whole idea of sucking a man's penis would have repelled her, but in thie marijuana inspired madness, she let her tongue wash slowly over the bluntly jabbing cock, tasting it with curiosity.

The seemingly insatiatable hunger in her stomach was starting to rise again like the wind on a stormy night, and once again the girl seemed to be falling into a kind of sexual trance where she was all body and no mind. Vorcaciously, she sucked on the unknown man's hardened cock, her tongue licking wildly as the blood engorged tip slashed furiously in and out between her tightly ovaled lips. In her confusion, she somehow understood that she had to suck him until he came, using her tongue and lips around his pulsating cock until he reached his shattering orgasm inside the cavity of her mouth.

"I'm going to shoot it in you baby, and I wanna see that throat of yours go up and down! Drain all of the cum out of me!" she heard him order from somewhere above her and his prediction came true a second later. The man who had been savagely pummeling her drenched and overworked cunt from behind suddenly gave a low pleasurable moan too and the girl tightened her ass cheeks as she felt his cock expand and grow more rigid deep up inside of her and then begin spewing its white hot sticky cum into her cock filled cunt. Her body jerked convulsively as he fucked into her, and in the same terrible moment, she instinctively increased the pressure of her lips on the man who was fucking her mouuth and his cock" then exploded furiously in response, sending a torrent of hot white cum into her warm, receptive, waiting mouth.

Her cheeks bellowed out like a ballon as the lewd male cum filled her warm mouth. She remembered his stern instructions and struggled not to lose a drop of the precious lustful liquid, gulping it all down as the wildly-ejaculating organ spurted against the roof of her mouth. He finally pulled his limp, deflating penis free of her cum coated lips as she swallowed the last of the pungent fluid and another man then immediately took his place.

Things became confused after that and Melanie lost track of who was fucking her or where she was being fucked. Orgasms followed one after another and often she would explode with ecstasy the moment a man entered her battered and bruised young body. Soon the men were coming back for seconds and when the marijuana finally caught up with her, the helpless young girl passed out....

## CHAPTER FIVE

After leaving Melanie Abbott at the bus station that night, Joe Brown had gone immediately to the apartment of his friends Rick and Susan who were living in a comfortable spacious apartment just off the campus grounds. They had invited him to stay permanently, using the spare bedroom, but after a couple of days, he had decided to leave and get a room in the men's dormitory. For one thing, Susan bore a striking resemblance to Melanie, and every time he looked at his friend's wife, she started him thinking about the girl he had met on the bus. This kept him in a continual state of depression. He had checked with the registar's office, asking for the address of a freshmen girl student named Melanie Abbott and they had informed him that there was no such person registered at the university. This had really thrown him into a turmoil.

What the hell had become of her? Had she been lying to him that day on the bus, merely pretending to be an incoming student? If so, why would anyone bother to do such a thing? And if she had not been lying, what on earth had happened to her? People don't just disappear! Yes, as a matter-of-fact, in places like Dallas, people disappear quite regularly, he reminded himself, and it was this that worried Joe most of all. If only he had not let her wander off on her own that night!

There was nothing to be done, of course. He had considered going to the police, but immediately recognized that this was foolish. More likely than not, they would laugh him out of the police station, and if the girl had really disappeared, her family and the university would all be looking for her. There was really nothing that he could do, except sit around and moon over her. That is precisely what he had spent a whole week doing, too!

Really, she had been the nicest looking girl he had ever seen and they could be having a real ball here together. Instead, he was sharing a room with two stupid guys Fred Doyle and Chuck Grant, both rich kids who were freshman students like himself. Naturally they were a few years younger than he since they were entering college fresh out of high school, and from the way they were acting they would probably remain "freshmen" throughout their entire four years of college.

They were both about equally loud and vulger, exactly the same kind of jerks Joe had learned to dislike when he was working on ships. They spent most of their evenings out carousing and drinking instead of studying, and then barged into their dorm as drunk as a pair of skunks, in the wee hours of the morning waking him up while he was trying to get a few hours sleep before an early morning class. The rest of the time, they talked about screwing girls in the most vulgar possible fashion, and in general, did everything they could think of to irritate the "old man," so they called him, who shared their room.

Now the weekend was coming up and he had two whole days staring him in the face! Two days of putting up with Fred and Chuck and their empty headed conversation about broads and booze. Rick and Susan were away for the weekend and he had a standing invitation to use their place, plus a key, so he could go there whenever he wanted, but somehow the idea of spending Friday night in an empty apartment depressed him even more than going out.

Fred was snoring noisily on the couch and Joe Brown looked at him balefully. The young man stayed up virtually all night, every night, banging in and out and disturbing Joe's sleep, and then made up for it by sleeping all the day himself and complaining bitterly whenever Joe snapped his pen. Chuck was out someplace, lining up dates for the night, and Joe longed for the moment when the two of them would take off for their evening's entertainment and leave him alone with his melancholy.

Damn! He thought angrily. If things had worked out properly, he could be headed out for an evening on the town with Melanie at his side. Maybe, if their romance had prospered, the two of them could have set up housekeeping together with Rick and Susan, who had, in fact, suggested that he find himself a girl and move in with them to share the expenses.

He heard heavy footsteps coming down the hall, and groaned inwardly, knowing that this was Chuck coming back to get his friend for their evening's adventures. Now there would be two hour's of commotion while the two of them shaved, changed their clothes, and bragged about all the wild sex they were going to get tonight. Then, finally, they would disappear and drink themselves into a stupor after it was all over.

"Wake up! Up!" proclaimed Chuck coming through the door with his customary crash. "I have something for ya that you are going to be wild about!"

"You'll have to excuse him," explained Fred, looking up sleepily from his couch. "The pressures getting to him, he's gone out of his mind!"

"Come on, up, up. I have made the greatest discovery ever made!"

"What is he talking about?" grumbled Joe, in no mood to listen to Chuck's nonsense.

"He's telling us we're going to get laid, I think," suggested Fred. "Alright, what the hell are you talking about."

"Aha, someone," continued the student, already a little drunk. "I have discovered the address of a house of the most ill repute. They have a most delictable little cunt, just primed and ready for a good fuck. We'll have her for the night if we get our asses over there right now."

"Will you guys get out of here!" snapped Joe with poorly concealed irritation. "I got fifty pages of this book to finish."

"The hell with books," said Fred, now fully awake now. "You spend so much time with your nose buried in those text books that I'm beginning to think that you're losing your touch with the ladies!"

"Yeah, come on, Joe," urged Chuck. "We've got to stay with this guy or somebody'll kill him."

"In his present condition, that somebody, would do mankind a noble service," answered Joe, but he was considering the proposition. He had vowed to himseelf that he would never again pay for it, and he was not about to go back on his promise now. The truth of the matter was that he had spent his whole first week on campus day dreaming about Melanie and studying like hell the rest of the time, and he knew absolutely no one in Dallas except these two jerks. Was an evening in their company better or worse than an evening alone? You could always go along for the ride and make sure that neither one of them got into trouble, he told himself. It would be dull, but he had to get out of this stifling dorm or face the prospect of going clear out of his mind.

"I'll go along to make sure that the two of you get back in one piece, but you'll have to take care of this spectacular dame on your own. I don't indulge when I have to pay for it."

"Hurrah, and keys to my car is yours for the night," raved Fred, tossing him the keys to his new Jaguar sports car. "My father has threatened to disown me if I total another car and I am not in the best of condition now for safe driving."

The standard two hours of preparations were shortened into one since his roommates were both anxious to get on the road, and by ten o'clock, Joe Brown found himself at the wheel of a sleek little sports car that deserved a better owner than Chuck Grant. The two other boys, by now slightly drunk, climbed in as well and Joe took off down the street.

"16 Angeles Court, is the appointed place, my good man. It's clear across town and watch out for the red lights and the boys in blue...."

That address, Angeles Court, rang a bell in Joe's mind, but he could not quite recall where he had heard it before, and after awhile he gave up trying. The neighborhood was distinctly on the seedy side and he worried about someone grabbing the car while they were inside, so he parked it under one of the few street lights which had not been broken. He locked it carefully before slipping the keys into his pocket and followed his two friends inside of Ruby's.

It was a medium slow night at Ruby's, since in the first week of Melanie's residence there, most of the regulars had come by to pay their carnal respects to her and afterwards had gone on their way to spread the word among their friends. A steady trickle of men had been coming and going all day, and Ruby and Gerome were satisfied, knowing that any new product takes time to become established on the market.

"Hi, fellows," Gerome called in a friendly greeting as the three young men walked into the lobby. "See you've heard about our new girl, eh?"

Fortunately Fred was now too drunk to do his imitation of a Texas cowhand, or Gerome would have thrown the three of them out on the street.

"Yeah, hear you've got a little gal here who really puts up a battle before you get to do your stuff," he remarked, wondering hus much this was going to set them all back.

"Twenty-five a throw, gents, and she's all yours. Gonna tackle her all three together or one at a time?"

"I'll sit this one out, if you don't mind," Joe said, looking at the big bouncer a little nervously. "If there's a bar around, I might like a drink while my friends are here uh ... visiting the young lady."

"One of them high and mighty types, eh? Well, I don't mind selling a little booze on the side. Make yourself comfortable, sport, and I'll have somebody bring you a drink. How 'bout you boys?"

"We've had ours, friend. Just lead us to that sweet young cunt!"

"Teamwork, eh? Maybe I'll join you and we'll make it a threesome?" Gerome offered, including himself uninvited in the party because he saw a chance to show off his masculine powers in front of these confident schoolboys. Then he turned to Joe. "If you get lonesome, kid, we'll be right down the hall in that end doorway there. No need to knock 'cause we're all friends here," he said to the good looking young man who had stretched out comfortably on the couch and located an old magazine to read while he waited for his roommates and he nodded to Gerome, breathing a sigh of relief as he disappeared down the hall with Fred and Chuck.

## CHAPTER SIX

Having tried almost every approach there was to the situation, but the scene always finished the same way, with her on the bottom being ravaged by every man who walked through the door. Melanie had finally given up any hope of escaping from this horrid place. The marijuana only made matters worse since she lost control completely whenever she smoked it and turned into the worst whore in the place. Without the marijuana, it was just plain hell, but she seemed to resist more and get beaten up worse as a result. Either way, the end was the same.

The imprisioned young girl paced back and forth in her room, wondering what day it was and whether or not she would ever get out of this place alive.

She had no idea what kind of plan Gerome might have in mind for getting rid of her, since it was obvioous he could not hold her prisoner forever. Or could he? Or, more likely, did he have a plan to silence her forever once her usefulness was ended? Now there was someone coming and she heard the key turn in the lock. You must go down fighting, she told herself. There's no other way! Resist until you die!

"Well, look at what we got here," sneered Fred as he stepped through the doorway, followed by Chuck and Gerome. "All undressed and nowhere to go."

It was a desperate maneuver, but Melanie knew she had to make her move while the door was still open and unlocked. If she could somehow fight her way past these three men, she would stand a chance of making it to the street. It made no difference that she was naked, since dozens of men had looked at every part of her naked body for the last week, and her sense of modesty was now somewhat dulled. She had to have her freedom at any cost!

"Hey! Watch out!" shouted Gerome, seeing that she still had some fight in her. The young girl had dashed for the door, her fingernails clawing at Fred's face and her knee swinging dangerously toward Chuck's unprotected groin. There was a few seconds of wild confusion and screaming by the door before the burly Gerome got his wits together and intervened decisively, slapping her brutally across the face and she fell back onto the bed.

"Told ya this one had some steam left in her," he gasped, nursing a long ugly scratch in his arm, where Melanie had clawed at him. "Okay, sonny, yer turn. Do your stuff!"

He patted Fred on the back, and the young man strode angrily forward, ashamed at having been caught so far off balance by a mere girl and anxious to even the score. He took two short running steps and then hurled his body through the air, knocking Melanie clear off the bed and landing on top of her on the floor. Melanie lay under him, the wind gone out of her for a minute, and her moment of resistance was gone and forgotten. The door was locked now and her opportunity had been lost. Gerome would not be caught off guard a second time.

Fred sat up on top of the naked girl, a cruel smile playing across his lips. The young man had a vicious streak of sadism deep inside of him, only partially covered by the expensive education paid for by his father. He had never had the opportunity to do exactly what he liked with a really good looking woman, but it was slowly occurring to him that this might be the chance he had been waiting for. So this one thought she was hot stuff eh? Well, Fred Doyle would show her who was boss. Those full pink lips of hers looked like they could use some action, and he knew just what to do with them!

Melanie closed her eyes and waited for her fate like an animal about to be slaughtered. The man was running his hands lasciviously all over her full voluptuous body, and she knew in advance that he would make it his business to humilate her as much as he could. She would pay for that little attempted escape, and then would pay again when Gerome got her alone with the whip.

"Little whore, you and I are going to play a very special game, I know," Fred informed her cruelly. "Get on your knees!"

It was hopeless and Melanie knew it. She was surrounded by three grown men who could make her do any perversely wicked thing they desired. She had no idea which particular perversion this one had in mind, but after awhile, all perversions seemed alike to her. After a week in the house, she had seen them all. She tried to cry out, but found that no tears would come. Even after such a short time there, she was getting hardened, getting used to abuse and maltreatment, and she realized with a pang of regret that she would never be that sweet innocent young coed she was, once upon a time. Even if she did manage to get out of this chamber of horrors alive, she would do as she was told now. Her display of bravado was over for today but perhaps tomorrow she would try again. Perhaps if she could really please one of her customers, make one of them fall in love with her, then someone might agree to take a note out with them for help or call the police.

"Take it out, baby," he commanded, indicating his fly. "I got a present in there for you."

Dully she moved to comply, fumbling a little with his belt buckle and then drawing down the zipper to reveeal a pair of white shorts. His pants fell to the floor and the young college boy stepped out of them and then made her remove his shorts. His long limp cock dangled obscenely between his legs, and Fred grinned down at her sadistically.

"Hmmm, I see that my little present isn't in the proper condition to be given away. Now well have to work on that, won't we little one?" As he spoke, the egoistical freshman slid his hands roughly into her long dark hair, tightening his grip so that he could move her head around as he desired, and also hurt her anytime he wished. With a sudden jerk, he yanked her face closer to his still flaccid penis.

"You're going to suck me now, baby," he commanded her. "I want to see you suck this cock of mine till I tell you to stop and not a moment before. You understand!"

Melanie understood. It was not he first time one of her customers had made this lewd request of her, but at those times she had been flying high on the marijuana and it had seemed easier to do, but now she was cold sober, and in full command of her faculties. The others had simply rammed themselves into her open mouth and had not asked her to do anything but endure it. But this man was forcing her to do it herself now and she didn't think that she could!

His hands tightened in her hair, reminding her that he still possessed the power to make her suffer whenever he wanted. Gerome had thrown himself comfortably on the bed and was watching with evil enjoyment. Chuck was straddling a chair and looking on with serious interest as if he were attending a scientific demonstration of some kind. Melanie opened her eyes to find that Fred's long slightly jerking cock was staring her right in the face, only inches from her delicate pink lips. Grinning like a devil, Fred reached down and rubbed the moist thick head of his slowly inflating penis against her cheeks, running it up over her nose and then down onto her mouth, never once loosening his grip on her soft, dark hair.

"Come on, baby, open up. Now, is the time!" he ordered her.

But Melanie felt as if her teeth were glued together. She wanted desperately to avoid any more pain, but something inside of her refused to cooperate in this lewd experiment, and her mouth remained solidly closed. Angered by this new show of resistance, Fred yanked again on her hair, forcing an offended cry to her lips. As soon as her mouth opened to protest, Fred made his move, jamming his lust bloated cock up into her mouth savagely. Her groan turned into a gurgle of distress as she felt the slowly hardening mass of male flesh plung into her mouth, almost choking her. Once inside, the man's penis began to expand as he excited himself by looking down at the gleaming blue veined shaft stuck obscenely in between her soft pink lips.

"Lets get to work, sweetheart," he warned her. "I want to see you suck!"

Knowing by bitter experience that he was in a position to enforce his wishes and would only hurt her again if she tried to rebel, Melanie started nibbling gently on his large flexible cock, feeling it become firmer and straighter by the moment as she caressed him with the sensual softness of her lips. The young man's eyes were almost bulging from his head as he looked down on the suffering, tormented young girl from his position of lofty superiority, watching her submissive mouth working slavishly over his rigidly throbbing cock. Fred jerked on her soft hair again just out of meanness, and was rewarded for this act of casual cruelty by seeing the girl react in fright, sucking his cruelly marauding instrument even deeper into the ravaged depths of her throat, sucking on him as if her life depended on it.

She decided to make him cum as quickly as possible and get it over with, hoping to please him enough so that he would refrain from hurting her more. She was using her tongue now, lashing back and forth against the sensitive nerve endings in his penis and making his hips flick involuntarily back and forth as he began to fuck slowly in and out of her widely stretched mouth.

Things were speeding up now, and the end was not far off. Fred was unbearably excited as he stood over the nakedly kneeling brunette like a reigning king, his hands twisting through the dark tangle of her hair, mumbling all the obscene words and phrases he could think of while he skewered mercilessly back and forth, frying to shove his jerking, over stimulated, instrument all the way down her gurgling throat.

## CHAPTER SEVEN

Joe finished the drink and glanced at his watch in utter boredom, having discovered that the magazine he had been reading was five years old. A few of the other prostitutes had wandered by and made a halfhearted attempt in interesting the good looking young man in their services, but Joe had merely smiled and shook his head. He was now contemplating ordering another drink to help him pass the time and wishing that he had thought to bring one of his textbooks along with him to study while it waited. It was stupid to have come anyway, he reminded himself sourly, how did you expect to get cheered up in the waiting room of a second class whore house? I would have been better off in my own room where at least it would be quiet. So he decided against the other drink, feeling that it might affect his studying tomorrow morning if he drank too much tonight. He got up off the couch to stretch his legs and began to pace back and forth. What the hell was keeping those guys? Nobody ever spent more than ten minutes with a girl in a place like this and his two rooommates had been in there for at least half an hour.

Oh yeah, he remembered, this was the girl who was supposed to put up some kind of fight before she gave in and let you get your rocks off. Joe shook his head in disgust. Not only did he dislike paying for it, but he had never been able to understand the kind of person wo liked to mix his sex life up with violence. What kind of jerk did you have to be to enjoy beating up a helpless girl? Clods like Fred and Chuck, was the answer, of course, and he mentally resolved that he was going to get himself transferred to another room as soon as it was possible.

But for the moment, he still had a real boredom problem and without thinking too much about the matter, he decided to stroll around and see how the two clowns were making out with this so called ball of fire. Ignoring a couple of the prostitutes, he meandered upstairs to the first door and stopped to listen. There was no sound, and Joe accurately guessed that the room had been sound proofed for some reason. Looking around him, he spotted another door which had been left open, and without much curiosity, he glanced inside, discovering to his surprise that the door led into a tiny compartment, just large enough for one person.

What the hell; he mused and stepped inside. It was a two way mirror and suddenly he understood everything. They had had deals like this in some places in South America as well for the people who thought that sex was a spectator sport. There the boys are now, he observed, and old Fred is having the time of his life with that gal, and she sure doesn't seem to be putting up much in the way of resistance. Joe could not see the girl's face, since it was buried in Fred's loins, but he whistled softly in admiration as he surveyed the voluptuous young body which knelt submissively before his roommate. Her breasts were really something, heavy and sensuous, and the rest of the body was a sight for sore eyes. This girl is really built, he thought, feeling a little tickle of sexual excitement in his own groin, as he watched her nakedly gleaming body being buffeted about as Fred fucked cruelly into her unwilling mouth.

"Ooohhh, suck it, suck it," he heard the younger man groan, his face contorted into a mask of pure passion as the girl inched him slowly but surely towards an orgasm. Joe felt slightly ashamed of himself for behaving like a voyeur, but the scene before him was really erotic and he could not tear his eyes away from the sight. Fred was moving

. around to the left now, bracing his back against the table, and in another moment Joe would be able to see the kneeling girl's face. With a body like that, he decided, it would be too much to ask for her to have attractive facial features as well, and then he saw her....

The shock almost knocked him back out of the hidden compartment, and for a moment the sturdy young man thought he was going to faint for the first time in his life. It was Melanie Abbott, that lovely dark haired girl he had met on the bus! So this is why she had never shown up at the university!

His eyes widening in shock and horror, Joe's mind searched for a reasonable explanation for this incredible appearance of the naive and apparently unsophisticated girl in the middle of this two bit brothel. He watched with amazement as the girl cooperated in her own defilement, energetically slavering over Fred's penis as if she had been sucking cocks all of her life, and like she would rather perform this lewd oral sodomy than anything else in the world. Each time the young student surged into her, Joe could see the smooth hard glistening flesh of Fred's penis sliding up into the warm moist cavern of her mouth puffing out her cheeks. He was really probing deeply now, his hands clamped on both sides of her head so that she could not escape or wiggle away at the critical moment when his warm sticky sperm would come gushing out of that unforgiving cock and flooded her innocent mouth.

Joe tightened his fists with rage. Of course, he told himself savagely. What a fool he had been! She had been putting him on royally that day during their bus ride together, pretending to be chaste and unsure of whether or not her hyman was still intact. How she must have laughed at him when he had accused her of being a typical small town virgin! And now the truth was out. She had obviously never had any intention of going to the university. She was headed for Dallas to make her fortune in a cheap whore house! No wonder she would not come with him to Rick and Susan's house that time, she couldn't make any money there!

For a moment, the unhappy young man stood indecisively, irrationally wishing he could burst into the room and beat up Fred and then slap Melanie around a bit too, for having cheated him like this. All the time he had spent worrying and day dreaming about her and all the time she was here in this place, having the time of her life!

But this was impossible, and he struggled to get ahold of himself. No, there was nothing to be done, and he couldn't even enjoy the satisfaction of walking out of this awful place into the clean night air, since he had the car keys and had to take Fred and Chuck back to school. And all the way home they would boast about the things they had done to this fantastic young whore. He could not bear the thought of listening to those two, but watching this lewd spectacle was even worse and the miserable man stumbled out of the concealed compartment and went back down the stairs to the parlor to resume his long wretched wait.

* * *

Fred looked down, a mood of savage joy passing through his mind, as he fucked ruthlessly into the girl's helplessly imprisoned face. There was nothing he liked better than completely humiliating and debasing a gal like this and he spat obscenity after obscenity down on her lewdly bobbing head as he speared into her like a madman. He had her where he wanted her now and his eyes gleamed as he watched the moist shaft of his cock disappearing into the tightly rounded oval formed by her invaded lips.

Melanie could feel the hard rubbery tip of his penis brushing lewdly against the back of her throat and her mouth was filled to overflowing with a lust inciting mixture of saliva and the pungent tasting fluid oozing from the tip of his swollen cock. The students hardened balls were beating steadily against her chin and she realized that he was almost there.

Then the student started to feel the familiar symptoms of an oncoming orgasm, the roaring in his ears and the hot burning sensation deep in his sperm filled testicles which told him clearly that he could not expect to hold out much longer. Fred thrust into her as deeply as he could, smiling as he heard her choke and gurgle for breath. At the same moment he pressed in with both his hands on her cheeks to increase the pressure on his hotly throbbing cock. A raging storm of sharp electric impulses seemed to be racing through his body and he gripped her head like a vise as he felt the savage rush of sperm begin. Great hot waves of fiery cum spurted forward from the warm repository of his balls and streamed out the lust bloated head of his cock into the back of her helplessly waiting mouth, filling her as she had never been filled before.

Melanie sputtered and gasped for a moment, but she knew instinctively that her labors were not yet finished. The spoiled young college freshmen was moaning sensuously above her as he emptied the obscene liquid from his loins into the warm moist sanctuary of her mouth, and she dutifully continued to suck on him until he commanded her to stop, gulping automatically as the viscous cum filled her mouth, not daring to risk offending him by spitting it out.

With a moan, he released her, allowing his slowly deflating cock to slip out from between her cum moistened lips, a thin string of the thick white cum still connecting the tip of her tongue to the jerking glands of his penis. The girl let her exhausted body go limp and she rolled helplessly back on the floor to await the next lewd, depraved act upon her defenselessly trapped body. Nothing mattered now, because they had done the worst thing possible to her and there could be nothing more savagely depraved than this! Even if they did it again and again, nothing could be as terrible as the first time, and she would get used to this, just like she had accustomed herself to having perfect strangers throw her on her back and plunge their long hard cocks up into her belly.

"Oh man, that was the greatest," gasped Fred as he stretched out on the bed, his again flacid cock still twitching moistly as he slowly recovered his sanity. "She's got a mouth like silk! I gotta do it again as soon as I get my hard-on back!"

"Only fifteen dollars for seconds," commented Gerome quickly, his keen commercial sense not blunted in the slightest by his growing sexual excitement. Were it not for the money involved, Gerome would have thrown these two creeps out long ago and used Melanie for his own lewd purposes, but he was in business to make some money, and that meant letting some of the others have their fun with her too. Besides, it provided a special kind of perverted excitement for him to watch another man abuse this young helpless creature, and his long hard cock was twitching with steadily growing stimulation.

"My turn," asserted Chuck quickly, getting up from his chair and approaching the girl. The young man had already stripped for action and his thin long cock was just as ready as he was, waving from side to side in front of him like a dividing rod as he walked. "And I want some of the same."

"Trouble with you college boys is that you got no imagination," commented Gerome suddenly, adjusting his pants to hide the enormous erection which had arisen in the past few minutes. "A couple of copycats!"

"What do you mean?" asked Chuck, pausing as he hovered over the nakedly submissive girl. "It's either fuck or suck, isn't it? Or have you invented a new way to do it?"

"There's another way, boys, but I didn't invent it. You ever try any of that rear end stuff?"

Chuck looked dubious for a moment, and then a slow lascivious grin broke across his cruel face. This was something he had never before had the opportunity to try with a girl, but from all that he had heard it was the ultimate in sexual pleasure for the man, although most women found it distinctly less enjoyable. It was something he had always wanted to have a go at, and this was his chance, perhaps the only opportunity he would ever have. He was not entirely clear about this girl's status in the whore house and she certainly did not resemble the usual prostitute in any way, but she seemed to have very little to say about what was done to her. Gerome was obviously the boss here, and if he said it was okay to tackle that nice tight little ass, then who was he to say otherwise?

"I might need some help, fellows," he decided. "She doesn't look too happy about the idea."

"She ain't got nottin' to say about it," growled Gerome with a warning look in Melanie's direction. "This little broad does what she's told to, or old Uncle Gerome gets real mean, don't he, honey?"

Melanie nodded dumbly, not entirely clear about what they were proposing to do to her. To her inexperienced ears, "rear end stuff" sounded as if Chuck intended to take her like a dog while she knelt on the bed. While none of this was pleasant, she actually preferred this position, since she did not have to look at her tormentor while he abused her. And at this point, her shame and humiliation were so complete that it hardly made any difference what lewd position they forced her into; there were no surprises let for Melanie Abbott, but she was wrong. There was one surprise left, something none of her other clients had dared to try with her. But by the time she realized what it was, it was too late to do anything about it.

"Grab her!" snapped Gerome, and the three men rushed forward like invaders storming a fortification. Before she could cry out, or argue with them, the girl felt herself being lifted bodily up into the air and was thrown on her stomach on the bed. She was so totally exhausted from the ordeal she had just been through she hardly bothered to resist. After all, what good could it possibly do to put up another fight at this stage of the game? There were three strong men in the room with her, any one of whom was tough enough to beat her into submission.

Without explaining what they were up to, Chuck positioned himself behind her up between her outstretched legs while Fred and Gerome lifted her hips up off the mattress, forcing her to kneel up with her sleekly rounded buttocks waving in the air while the two men pinned her shoulders to the surface of the bed.

"Get her arms over her head," ordered Gerome. "We don't want no interference once junior gets going here. And that little cherry don't look like it's gonna be all that easy to get through."

Slowly but surely it began to filter through Melanie's innocent mind that this was not going to be merely another unfeeling assault on her tortured vagina. They were after something much more depraved this time and she was once again afraid of what they were about to do to her.

"Don't hurt me," she pleaded, knowing in advance that anything she said would only make matters worse.

"Now don't you worry about a thing, dear," Chuck reassured her
unconvincingly. "We're just trying to further your education, and widen
your ... uh ... your outlook on things. Don't tell me this is the first time
you've gotten it in the ass?"

Melanie's mind was stricken by a sudden paralysis as she digested these
vicious words. She had been prepared mentally and physically for almost
any other torture they chose to inflict upon her, but this was absolutely
unheard of. It wasn't even natural! It was inhuman! Surely the man was just
trying to frighten her, to scare her! He wanted her to plead and beg for
mercy and then pretend to change his mind and penetrate her in the usual
way. My God, he couldn't really mean it!

However, she failed to convince herself that Chuck was kidding and
instinctibly she tightened her buttocks together protectively, and the terror
of the thought sending shudders of fear through her soft quivering young
body. They'll kill me, she told herself in the darkest despair. They're going
to keep me here forever and ever, just doing worse and worse things to me
until someone goes too far and I die. And this could be the time right now!

"Oh baby, have you ever got the most beautiful little ass I have ever laid my
eyes on!" proclaimed Chuck blissfully. "And I intend to lay more than my
eyes on it before I'm finished."

Melanie clenched her teeth as she felt his hard demanding hands on the
flacid half moons of her buttocks, separating the tightly clenched cheeks
with brute force and his fingernails dug cruelly into her soft delicate flesh as
he struggled to open up her ass cheeks. Melanie did her best to resist, but
her position was not really suitable for fighting off this kind of depraved
attack, and suddenly, cruelly, he spread her apart until she could feel the
warm air in the room blowing gently over the tiny unprotected little anal
opening.

"Oh man, that's some tight ass she's got there!" Chuck muttered, having
given her helplessly upturned rectum a careful inspection. "Hold on tight,
fellows, I'm going to prepare the way a little."

With the tip of his middle finger he probed at the nakedly defenseless
entrance to her virginal young rectum. Melanie tightened the puckered little
lips on a final effort to avoid the inevitable. She knew it was coming anyway
despite her frantic efforts to protect herself, but somehow she could not

force her terror stricken body to relax and accept this final degradation. Chuck probed persistently, running his saliva moistened finger around the tight elastic circle to tease her a little, and then pushed forward unexpectedly, sinking the finger in as far as the first knuckle and forcing an anguished cry to her lips. The pain was not as acute as she had feared, but the humiliation was every bit as unbearable as she had imagined it would be. There she was, spread out on her hands and knees, her smoothly rounded buttocks stuck obscenely up in the air and her full womanly breasts crushed into the mattress below while this young maniac pushed his fingers into the delicate interior of her unprotected little anus.

She hoped he would be satisfied with what he had already done and go no further, but she was dealing with a most unpleasant young man, and his perverted lusts had not yet begun to be satisfied. This was only the first step and there must be many more to follow. Melanie relaxed a little, weary from the effort of concentrating so much energy in one part of her body and the boy seized the opportunity to worm a second finger along side of the first. This time it really hurt and her body convulsed in agony despite the two strong men who were holding her tightly.

"Oh please don't do that," she begged piteously. "It's ... it's just awful!" It seemed like a ridiculous thing to say, and the three heartless men evidently thought so too, since the room was filled with roars of cruel lascivious laughter.

"Oh, of course it's awful," repeated Chuck, mimicking her refined, out of state accent. "That's why we like to do it. We're awful people!"

For the first time in several days, Melanie felt that she was really able to cry at last, even though crying was not going to do the slightest bit of good in her present circumstance. So they had not been kidding her. This degenerate young man was really going to make love to her back there! And to think that a few minutes ago it never would have occurred to her that such an unspeakable thing was even possible. Why hadn't her parents ever told her about such things?

Melanie wiggled desperately, gyrating her buttocks from side to side in one last attempt to break away from him, but Chuck controlled her easily, digging his fingers into the soft vulnerable flesh of her smooth white hips while he worked his two fingers in and out of the dark moist anal hole trying to widen it enough to make his entrance.

"Now we're getting somewhere," he commented calmly, digging into her virginal rectum one last time and then yanking his fingers out with a sudden jerk. "I'm ready to roll, friends, hold on tight to her! Here I go!"

Forcing her knees still farther apart with his muscular legs, Chuck dropped his head down between the quivering cheeks of her buttocks and moistened the tiny little anus with his tongue in order to lubricate the small elastic circle and make it easier for his cock to slide inside. He was already over excited at the prospects of bringing off this lewd sodomistic invasion, and Melanie could feel his body shaking with sexual stimulation behind her as he lapped at her like a dog and her anus throbbed in terror of what was to come.

She was helpless now, ready to be pierced and Melanie felt his hands clasp firmly on her hips in order to hold them still as he maneuvered his long thick dagger-like cock into position for the obscene impalement. The huge throbbing cock pressed lightly at the tiny entrance, and another tremor of shock raced coldly through the girl's abused young body. It seemed too large, much larger than it had looked a few minutes before when she had caught a glimpse of him coming toward her. The experiment was doomed to failure in advance, she decided with relief, because he could never get that huge thing up inside of her. Certain things were simply impossible!

But Chuck was not ready to concede defeat, although he, too, was wondering if Gerome's suggestion was really practical. He placed his thumbs directly into the deep quivering crevice and began stretching the small puckered little circle which was barring the tiny entrance to her rectum. The flesh was rubbery and resistant beneath his fingers, but bit by bit he could feel it yield as he applied a steadily increasing pressure.

"Noooooooooooooooh!" she groaned, knowing that the worst was yet to come. "Pleasssssssse! I'll do anything you ask, but not this."

"You'll do anything we ask, and this too, young lady!" Gerome grinned down at her, as Chuck rammed his long desire hardened cock into the tightly clasping crevice and began to apply deadly pressure to the nether entrance to her body. Melanie screamed as she felt the pain mount, but no one was listening to her agony, and she herself was only conscious of the sharp relentless pressure against her. The tightly resisting ring held tight for as long as the strength of her frail muscles would permit, and then they surrendered and the room echoed with a loud obscene popping sound as the bulbous tip of his cock slipped up inside of her cringing little asshole.

"Oh Christ, it's tight!" moaned Chuck from behind her, but she hardly heard this mild complaint as she was completely engrossed in her own problems. Worse than the actual pain, which was unbearable by itself, was the mental anguish of knowing what was happening to her. The terrible penetration of this man's death dealing organ was vibrating through her body like an earthquake, and her painfully wide spread rectum felt as if a great solid log had suddenly been rammed up inside of it, stretching every tortured fiber of her widely dilated anal passage to the breaking point. It hurt her to scream, so she merely grunted in grief and horror, wiggling futilely in a hopeless attempt to break away from this rear guard action.

He wanted the whole experience of violating a woman ami ally so Chuck pushed again, not satisfied with merely embedding the tip of his rigid thickened cock up inside of the unnatural sanctuary of her helpless rectum. She grunted again as he wormed steadily up into her, pushing the tender anal flesh inside of her ahead of his cruelly advancing cock until his heavy sperm filled balls slapped noisily against the soft hair covered lips of her neglected unfilled cunt below.

She was pierced, penetrated, skewered like a wild animal on a spit, and the man's huge cudgel filled her anus like a cork forced into an already opened wine bottle.

Chuck was beside himself with excitement by the depraved sensuality of this lewd sodomy, and the student hovered over her tormentedly kneeling body, growling at her every vile obscenity which came into his evil brain. Melanie had never felt so humiliated in all the days of her life as he began slowly but surely sawing in and out of her, using the delicate internal flesh of her rectum for his own selfish carnal pleasure. The long punishing rod glided through her narrow clasping hole with smooth tormenting strokes, pulling tiny ridges of pink flesh out with it on the out stroke just as if he were in the process of turning her inside out. Melanie could hear Gerome and Fred snickering lewdly above her and even though she could not see them, the anguished girl could feel the stern pressure of their rough hands on her shoulders as they pressed her harshly into the bed.

She had never felt so entirely helpless! She was pinned like a butterfly in someone's collection, and held slavishly in this degrading kneeling positiion like a beaten slave prostrate before the master. Despite the fact that the two men were practically sitting on her, Melanie's body began to quiver and shake uncontrollably every time Chuck seared into her with an extra hard lunge. She could hear him grunting and moaning with pure animal pleasure behind her, and hated herself for involuntarily giving him so much enjoyment when she would much rather have killed him on the spot. If she could somehow get back at him for what he was doing to her now! If only there were some way to make him cry out with pain too!

## CHAPTER EIGHT

Sitting on the sofa in the waiting room, Joe Brown realized that he was glancing at his watch every few minutes. Face it, you clod, he was telling himself savagely. You fell in love with the little whore, didn't you. You had your whole life all planned out and you just included her into your future without thinking about the possibility that she wouldn't fit in. You thought that she was too innocent to be allowed to walk the streets alone, but you were mistaken. Damn! It's you who belong back in grammar school!

On top of everything else, the young ex-sailor was sexually aroused, bothered by a hard throbbing erection inside of his pants that would not go away and could not be ignored. The scene upstairs of Melanie Abbott humbly crouching on her knees and accepting Fred's long hardened penis up into the warm moist haven of her mouth, had made a permanent impression on him, a scene he would remember for the rest of his days.

You could go in and get a piece of that too, he advised himself lewdly. You could get in line behind Chuck and fuck her until she screamed for mercy. You owe yourself something for what she's put you through! A little revenge might help you forget ... But he shook his head in sorrow. No, this was impossible. She might be a whore, but he could never face her again and if he made love to her, he might find himself more hopelessly entangled with her than before. Imagine falling in love with a whore!

"Hey baby, you gonna sit here all night alone?"

Joe had been so involved with his own dark thoughts that he had not heard the woman walk barefoot into the room, and he jumped a little when he heard her voice.

"Ah, I didn't mean to upset you, honey," she soothed him. "It's just friendly little Sarah, come in to see if she couldn't help you with your problem. Come on up to my room, lover boy and we'll see if we can't cure your problem and get that nasty frown off your handsome face."

Caught off guard, Joe smiled back at the woman as he looked her over. She was at least ten years older than he was, and had the free and eash manners of a girl who has spent most of her adult life within the walls of a brothel, but Sarah had taken the trouble to preserve her figure and her looks, knowing that they constituted her only means of livelihood. In her thirties, she was still supple and sexy looking, particularly with what she was wearing at this moment, which consisted merely of a black lacy bra, frilly nylon panties and long black stockings.

Joe went through a short and losing battle with his conscience. All right, he had vowed he would never again go to bed with a prostitute, but this was surely a special example. There he was, his heart broken and his cock standing up like the Eiffel Tower and what else was he supposed to do? Maybe this gal could cheer him up a little, help him to forget about Melanie Abbott.

"Anything you like, honey," she encouraged him gently, smiling in his direction as if she understood exactly what he was thinking about. "Just close your eyes and pretend it's a girl you'd really like to be in bed with."

That did it. Joe got to his feet, flashed her a sheepish grin, and the two of them walked hand in hand up the old creaky stairs to Sarah's room.

"What would you like me to do, lover?" she asked him seductively as he reached deftly behind her to unfasten her black bra and free her heavy sensuous breasts. Joe felt his cock jerk instinctively in his pants as her large brown nipples tumbled free of their confinement, and her eyes dropped to the front of his pants. "Huummm, I see we're all ready. What were you waiting for down there, honey, an engraved invitation. Come on over here."

She was really a nice girl, Joe decided, even if she was a professional, and the young man felt his body relax as he dropped his pants on the floor. For some reason, he felt at ease with her, like she was an old friend to whom he could talk without embarrassment.

"I came here with a couple of guys," he confessed. "They're down entertaining themselves with your colleague, Melanie."

"Yeah, I might have guessed," said Sarah. "So you were waiting for your turn to ... hey, how come you know her name? Is she that well known already?"

"Nah, I ran into her on the bus coming here to Dallas. I didn't even know she was a ... I mean, I didn't realize that she was in this profession."

"She wasn't then," giggled Sarah vaguely, bending over to strip off the flimsy nylon panties and then turned around to face him, stark naked except for her long black stockings. "And I wish somebody'd put her back on that bus to wherever she came from! I haven't had a customer in a week.

I know the boss is getting rich off that little broad, but she's ruining our morale in this place like mad. Whoever heard of a one girl whore house?"

At this point, Joe ceased to think very clearly for a moment because Sarah's arms had gone around his neck and she was pressing her full voluptuous breasts into his chest and kissing him with a fair imitation of genuine passion. Or perhaps, he wondered, it was real passion. After all, she hasn't had a man in a week and these gals probably need it worse than anyone. He tumbled her over backwards onto the bed and crawled over her waiting, willing body when the next thought struck him.

"What do you mean when you say she probably wasn't a prostitute when I met her?" he demanded, an ugly suspicion creeping over him, "Why did she come here if she wasn't already a prostitute?"

"That's the big question, baby," Sarah giggled, her hand snaking agilely down the front of his undershorts to stroke the thick smooth foreskin of his rising hardness. "I don't guess it was her idea, and maybe Gerome used some muscle. Well, I'll be giving away some company secrets in a minute if I ain't careful."

"Give away some secrets," Joe urged her. "If she wasn't a whore before, how did she get to become one so fast? Come on, baby, talk, I want to know!"

The call girl's face froze as she realized that her youthful client was serious and she did her best to make him forget about the dark haired captive on the floor below them. Moving quickly, she rolled Joe over on his back, her head diving in the direction of his loins.

"Let's suck," she proposed obscenely. "I'll make you real happy down there and you can close your eyes and pretend I'm Melanie if you want to. I don't mind at all."

"I want to do more than think about Melanie," the young man snarled, seizing the older woman by the hair and dragging her parted lips away from his excited cock. "I want to know more about her. Was she brought here by force?"

"I'll tell you two things, Mister," Sarah spat back at him, starting to lose her temper with this difficult young client. "First of all, she walked in here of her own free will, and secondly if you hurt me, Gerome is gonna beat the hell out of you. I'll fuck or suck or do just about anything else a woman can do, but if you wanna work out your agressions, do it someplace else ... not on me!"

"Answer one more question," Joe said, lowering his voice and realizing that he had made a tactical error. "Is she here of her own free will? Can she walk away anytime she wants to?"

I told you those were company secrets!" snapped the older woman shaking his hand out of her hair and looking him straight in" the eye. "Look, did you come up here to get laid or ask questions?"

Joe made his decision and executed it in the same instant, hurling the prostitute onto her back and grabbing his belt up off the floor. Working fast and expertly, he forced her resisting wrists together and quickly tied her to the top of the bed, then ducking down to the floor again to use one of her own stockings to tie her legs together so that afterwards the woman was helplessly bound.

"Now you listen to me. I haven't learned much in my life so far but I have discovered a couple of ways to make people real talkative. I want the whole story about that girl, or I'm going to make you sorry. Now do your talking!"

"You can go to hell!" spat Sarah, enraged at the position he had put her in.

Joe smiled back at her with a harsh thin grimace and reached for his pack of cigarettes. He lit one and sat down on the bed next to her, using his free hand to stuff her panties into her open mouth. Then he took a deep breath and ran the lighted end of the cigarette quickly from one quivering nipple down into the crevice between her two trembling breasts, and then up to the other nipple.

"AAAAAAAHHHHH!!" she groaned, her voice muffled by the panties that were stuffed in her mouth and a thin red line rising on her naked chest where the young man had trailed the fiery cigarette.

"Oh, you bastard," she gasped as soon as he had removed the panties from her mouth. "Gerome is gonna kill you for this and I will help him!"

"Gerome is someplace else but I'm here with the cigarette in my hand. I know a lot of interesting places to put a cigarette, lady, and I'm going to start experimenting if you don't start talking. Is Melanie being held a prisoner here?"

Sarah looked at him with pure hatred, her teeth clamped together resolutely and Joe realized that he was dealing with a very tough customer. He shifted his position and slowly parted her curly brown triangle of moist pubic hair with his fingers as if he were preparing to caress her again. Then he carefully moved the lighted cigarette in the direction of her tiny hard clitoris.

"I can't imagine anything that would hurt worse than this," he warned her. "You feel like talking before I do it or after?"

"Wait," she sobbed, fear finally sweeping over her as she saw exactly how far he was prepared to go to get this information. "For God's sake, don't burn me down there!"

"Then talk!"

"Gerome will kill me if I tell you."

"I'll kill you if you don't!"

"Okay, okay, but please take that terrible cigarette away."

"I'm listening, woman, but I'm not hearing anything."

"Alright, listen then! The girl came in here by mistake I guess she thought this was a hotel. Ruby was against it, but Gerome got the kid stoned on pot the first night and fucked her himself. Then he decided she could be good for the business and they have kept her locked up in that room ever since. I knew it was gonna lead to trouble, but they wouldn't listen to me."

"Then she's a prisoner? She never wanted to be a prostitute?"

"Hell no! She's supposed to be going to the university in town but they made her write a letter to the school saying she wasn't coming and another one to her parents, so nobody'd look for her for awhile, but they can't keep her here forever, I told 'em!"

"So what were they going to do with her after she's all used up?" Joe insisted, knowing the answer in his head, but wanting to have his worst suspicions confirmed.

"Man, I don't have to draw you a picture, do I?

After the novelty has worn off, they'd have to get rid of her, you know."

"How would they get rid of her, let her go?"

"What would you do in Gerome's shoes? If he let her go free and she decided to go to the police, he'd spend the rest of his life in prison for kidnapping. He'd have to take her for a long ride down to the Gulf. A lotta bodies manage to turn up in the ocean and nobody asks too many questions. Please get that damn butt away from my cunt, Mister, I've told you everything I know. Listen, don't let anyone know I talked to you, please, or Gerome would throw my body in after her."

"Okay, listen," Joe ordered, thinking fast. "If you want to get out of this with your skin in one piece, you get dressed now and get out of this place as fast as you can move."

"But Gerome will...."

"Gerome isn't going to bother you or anybody else again because I am going to kill him, do you understand?"

"Y ... Yes," she sobbed faintly.

"And if you try to warn anyone, I'm going to kill you too. Do you have the picture?"

Sarah's will to resist was completely broken. This sad faced man had suddenly been transformed into a savage wild man, and she realized that he might really be capable of doing all that he said he would. Gerome was a rough ugly customer, but this man was twenty years younger and his mind was now clouded by drink or maybe drugs. She nodded dumbly and Joe loosened the knots in her stockings and helped her to her feet. Sarah quickly scrambled into her clothing, slipping a sweater and slacks on over her scanty bra and panties and them Joe followed her back down the stairs to the deserted waiting room to make sure she went straight out the front door. He hated to take the chance involved in letting loose for fear she would try and warn the others in the house, but harming a reasonably innocent working woman like Sarah was too much for him and he decided that the risk had to be taken.

She turned as she stood by the door to the street, her hand on the knob.

"Good luck, fellow," she whispered faintly. "He's got it coming to him."
Then she turned and disappeared into the night.

Upstairs, as she surged back against the cruel young man who was
sodomizing her brutally from behind, Melanie gritted her teeth and praying
all the while for the strength to do what she had to do. Slowly at first, and
then with more energy, she began to undulate her body, swingin her hips in
tiny rotating circles and putting all the pressure she could on Chuck's
laboring cock.

"She's starting to turn on," he crowed happily, mistaking her desperate
efforts to end it for him as the beginning of lust on her part. He groaned
and skewered into her with renewed energy, exciting himself beyond
endurance with the sight of this gorgeous young girl kneeling humbly
before him, a victim of anything he chose to inflict upon her. There was not
an ounce of resistance left in her innocent young body now and she was his
property to batter and abuse as much as he wanted.

Melanie's head thrashed from side to side on the mattress and Gerome and
Fred had both released their hold on her arms, realizing that she was
beyond fighting back at this point. Her long silken hair lashed back and
forth like a thousand tiny whips and her body bucked and heaved like a
mad woman's as she lewdly encouraged him to end it all and fill her moist
nether crevice with his hot merciless cum.

Chuck was nearing the end of the best ride in his life and then he gripped
the tops of her thighs, his sharp fingernails digging into her delicate flesh as
he pounded in and out of her with all the might he could muster from his
body, being motivated by a sadistic wish to make her moan with agony.

"Aaaaaggghhh!!" she obliged him by moaning piteously beneath him as he
flicked deeply into her tortured anus. "Ugggh!"

But it was almost over and Melanie could feel the cruel student's cock
expanding and growing as if he were having a second erection on top of the
first. A week ago she would have been mystified by this phenomenon, but a
lot of education had been crammed into this seven days, and now she
understood that the man was about to cum into the unnatural receptable of
her anus.

"Oh cum, please cum," she begged him miserably, fucking her widely split buttocks back into his loins as hard as her pain wracked body would permit. Chuck gasped above her, incoherent words tumbling from his lips and then he felt the hot steaming cum begin to erupt from deep within his lusting balls, searing up through his penis and out into the narrow ravaged channel of her anal passage. Sighing and moaning with delight, he bucked into her endlessly, emptying his hot cum in the moistened crevice of her buttocks until there was no more to spill out.

"Oh man, that was the greatest ... wow!" he said as he crudely jerked his limp, already deflating penis from the overflowing little hole of her rectum, but Fred cut him off with an urgent remark.

"Wait! I smell smoke!"

"Damn it, what the hell can that be?" quiered Gerome looking alarmed. One of the problems involved in running an illegal operation like this cat house was the fact that you had to handle your own emergencies. You could hardly call the fire department or the police to help out.

"This place is on fire! Shit!" exclaimed Chuck, sniffing the air and then climbing rapidly into his pants. "Let's get outa here before the whole damn fire department arrives!"

The emergency shook Melanie out of her daze and she sat up on the bed, feeling a brand new fear sweep over her. The heat from the hall was already starting to be noticeable in the room and the two college boys dashed out of the room, leaving Gerome behind to deal with the situation.

"Get my clothes," Melanie pleaded as the big burly man glaned out in the hall to find himself confronted by a roaring fire coming from the end of the corridor. There was no problem about getting out, he realized, because the stairway was still clear down to the street, but Ruby's was going up in smoke! There was no way to put out the fire and it would soon burn the building to the ground ... and fast!

"Please don't make me run naked out into the street," Melanie begged, getting off the bed and running towards him with her hands outstretched for mercy. But Gerome was doing some hard thinking about her at that moment. The fire department and even the police could already be on their way, and it was time for him to disappear. Everyone else could be counted on to keep their mouths shut and they could open the brothel somewhere else, but if the cops caught him carting a naked screaming girl down the street, there would be some unpleasant questions to answer and he didn't want to be around.

"You ain't goin' nowhere," he snarled, pushing her roughly back onto the bed and fumbling in his pocket for the door key. They would find her ashes in the morning, he told himself, and the bones that remained are hard to identify. This saved the trouble of doing it later.

A lithe fast moving figure was emerging from the hidden compartment behind the two way mirror carrying a broom stick and because of the confusion and his haste, Gerome could not react fast enough to recognize the face as belonging to the shy student who had elected to wait behind in the parlor and so he dismissed the figure as being of no importance. He turned his back on him and addressed himself to the problem of getting the door securely locked. It was a fatal move.

The broom stick is a deadly weapon when it is used by an expert and Gerome felt it spearing into the small of his back, numbing him and sending his big body hurling into the tiny room where the naked girl sat trembling on the edge of the bed. Before Gerome could even get his head turned, Joe had followed him into the room and hit him again on the back of the neck, stunning him into semi-consciousness. The key to the sound proofed room fell free from his limp fist and Joe scooped it up.

"My clothes," Melanie whimpered. Everything was happening too fast for her to understand and she could only think about having to race through the streets of Dallas stark naked.

"No time to look for them," Joe barked, and he snapped the sheet off the bed and wrapped her bareness in it. Seeing that she was too dazed to move, he threw her over his shoulder like a sack of potatoes and ran into the hall pausing there to lock the door to the soundless room from the outside.

"There's a fire!" moaned Melanie, now half out of her mind from fear and exhaustion.

"I know, baby, I started it," the young man responded and then carried ger gently away from the burning building and hell!

"You'll be much more comfortable here," Joe said to Melanie tenderly, tucking in the covers of the bed and turning off the light in the bedroom.

"Try to sleep, Melanie, you've been through a lot lately."

With her dark head protruding from the clean pastel sheets and a puzzled smile on her pale face, the girl looked more like a frightened child than a young woman who has just survived a week's enslavement in a brothel. Joe hesitated a minute and then bent quickly to kiss her cheek in a brotherly fashion. He would have like nothing more than to throw back the blankets and climb in with her, but he knew that that was out of the question for the evening or possibly, forever. Who knows, he asked himself unhappily. After all that she's been through she may never like sex again, and every time she looks at me she may remember that horrible experience. He guessed that only time would tell.

Stripping off his clothing in the bathroom, he treated himself to a nice warm shower before climbing into his bed on the couch. A lot of things had gone right. It had been fortunate that he had had the keys to the sports car in his pocket when they had burst out of the burning building in the darkened street, the sound of the sirens already ringing in their ears. Chuck and Fred had fortunately disappeared somewhere and he had been able to stuff the dazed youngg girl into the car and get her away from the scene of the crime before the fire trucks and police arrived.

The second piece of good luck had been the fact tha Susan and Rick were away for the weekend, providing him with a comfortable safe place to bring Melanie to recover. They had almost been seen by a curious neighbor when he had carried her prostrate figure into the apartment, but good luck had been on their side again and there was no one else around to see the sight of him carrying the body of a sheet draped girl into the deserted apartment.

Joe walked naked into the living room where he had thrown a blanket over the couch and prepared to make himself comfortable for the night. He flipped on the radio, hoping for some relaxing music as he smoked a cigarette and was rewarded by soft romantic music. He crawled under the cover and tried to relax, feeling the tension drift away from his body despite the lingering feeling of desire which had been with him the entire evening.

"We interrupt this broadcast to bring you a news bulletin," the announcer said and Joe reached for the radio, not particularly interested in a news bulletin this late in a long and hard evening. "Police report that Ruby's Hotel, 16 Angeles Court, Dallas has been totally destroyed by a sudden, three alarm fire. Only a few guests were staying in the hotel at the time of the blaze and there was no loss of life except for the presumed fatality of the hotel's general manager, Mr. Gerome Ives, who was known to be inside the building when the violent fire broke out, and has not yet been located by the local police. Miss Sarah Green, a former employee of the hotel, stated that the cause of the fire could have been a pile of oily rags which were stored in a closet on the second floor. Mrs. Ruby Hall, the owner of the destroyed building, suggested that careless smoking in bed may have been the reason for the fire, but noted that the hotel was insured for its full value, and would be re-opened at a new location in the very near future. Speaking of the presumed death of her manager, Mr. Ives; Mrs. Hall stated that he had been a fine upright man who was a credit to the hotel industry.

Joe snapped off the radio with a snort, not entirely upset by the news. He was not yet so hardened about life that the knowledge that he had killed a man failed to affect him, but if anyone deserved to die it was Gerome. That man had fully intended to leave Melanie inside that burning building. It was poetic justice that he had been left there in her place.

"Joe?" came a soft quavering voice from the next room.

"Yeah, honey, are you okay?" .

"I'm feeling better, thank you, but where are you going to sleep?" Melanie wanted to know.

"Here on the couch, Melanie. Don't worry about me, I'll be fine."

"Joe, I'm sorry to bother you so, but I'm still a little frightened and I hate to see you sleeping on the couch." Her voice trailed off and the young man could hardly believe his ears.

"Are you frightened, would you like me to come in with you?" he asked, barely concealing his rising excitement from his voice.

"After everything that's happened my modesty isn't very important anymore," stated the girl, her voice stronger and more resolute now. "The bed is big enough for two."

Melanie lay absolutely still as she felt the mattress give under Joe's weight and she felt the added warmth in the bed as another body stretched out next to hers. Instinctively, she turned, hardly conscious of the fact that they were both naked, and sheltered herself in his strong arms. Making love was the farthest thing from her mind, but she needed to be held by someone who cared and she could trust, someone who would not hurt her and she had found him.

"I'm glad I found you again," he said simply, his voice coming to her in the dark as if a disembodied ghost had spoken. There was no need for her to reply. She had already confessed how glad she was to see him again, but she shivered as she realized that she was lying in the arms of a man who had deliberately killed someone that very night. My education is proceeding very rapidly, she thought. A week ago, I wasn't really sure whether I was even a virgin or not. Now that issue is settled forever and I'm in bed with a person who can kill people when he needs to. I've come a long way in that time.

His hands were stroking her back softly, running from the nape of her neck down to the base of her spine where her lush well rounded buttocks began to rise. Between their bodies, pressed against her stomach, she could feel the hardness of his fully aroused manhood, and the sensation sent a tremor of excitement through her body.

"Joe, she began hesitantly. "Joe, when we first met, I really didn't know which end was up. You told me I was a typical small town virgin and you were right."

The young lover, said nothing, knowing that she had something important to tell him and deciding to let her get it out in her own way.

"But, well, you can imagine what happened to me all last week. Just being raped isn't all that important, really, I mean it isn't even a sin if you don't want to do it and usually I didn't, so it was just humiliating and sometimes it hurt; but other times the men just came and did things to me. You must know what kinds of things they did, and they forced me to like it and ... I reacted and did like it! I'm sorry, because I'm not really good enough for you anymore, Joe. I can see now that you wanted me so bad that first night we met and I thought I was too good for you. Now it's changed and I'll always be a little bit of a prostitute for the rest of my life."

"Its okay, honey," he soothed her. "That's all over now, don't worry."

"No, it'll be part of me forever," she insisted, her voice quivering with emotion as she wrapped her arms more tightly around his neck. "Anyway, this is what I am trying to say. You came to Ruby's tonight looking for a prostitute, I think. Well, you have really found one, Joe. I am yours to do with as you want ... and you know, I can't wait."

Joe started to explain that he had not been looking for a prostitute tonight, but the thought drifted off as he felt her body melting into his. Melanie began to shiver when she felt his hands coursing more boldly over the soft lines of her young exciting body. She was finally his for the taking. There was no further need for coy adolescent conversation, she was now fully a woman, ready to give her all to the man who had saved her. She was too pure inside ever to be dirtied by the likes of Ruby and Gerome and all of those other men, and he realized that she was offering him something that had never been offered freely by her to anyone else. In a way, she was a virgin again, and he was to be her first lover.

Almost trembling despite his past experience with women, the excited young man hovered over her on his knees, letting her eyes rest calmly on the long hard shaft of his fully erected penis and running his hands greedily over the softly yielding flesh of her soft breasts and stomach, and then to her slim white thighs and the moist inviting "vee" which was so plainly being offered up to him in sacrifice. Melanie closed her eyes as the now familiar waves of pleasure washed over her sensitive body, but this time it was different, she was in the arms of someone who loved her ... someone who cared ... and she was at peace.

He feared, for a few minutes, that she had drifted off into her own private dream world and wanting to ease her back to reality, he bent and kissed her tenderly on the lips, feeling her react immediately by the spearing of her tongue hotly up into his open mouth. No, there was no queston about it, she was with him every inch of the way, and Joe took advantage of the intimate moment to send his hungry fingers into the warm wet core of her abused young body.

"Oh, oh, Ooohhh!" she sighed contentedly as he gently massaged the tender inner flesh of her slowly clasping vagina, finding to his satisfaction that she was thoroughly moist and wet, and he knew that she now wanted this as much as he did! But Joe could hardly believe that his mind was telling him. After all, he hardly knew her, only spending two or three hours with her on the bus a week before and about the same amount of time together with her tonight. They hardly knew each other, really, and she had spent seven long days and nights being raped and manhandled in every conceivable fashion during that time. Yet, somehow, she wanted him and wanted him badly!

He decided there was no point in postponing this pleasure another instant and he covered her warm receptive body with his own, feeling the tiny hardened tips of her nipples digging fiercely into his chest as he spread himself over her like an all engulfing cloud. He could sense the wild uncomfortable excitement building in her body and her hands slithered between their two writhing bodies to caress the throbbing tip of his erect penis with agile and now expert fingers. This much he had hardly expected, but it was all true. She seemed to have learned in one week in a brothel the full science of sex that it had taken him years to master. Who knows, he grinned to himself, maybe she can teach me a few things I haven't even learned yet!

Now she was arching her pelvis up to meet him, clearly inviting him to worm his long desire ridden rod into the warm moist recesses of her cuntal depth, and he was beside himself with sensual excitement. For a moment, Joe was tempted to oblige her and come crashing into her vagina, but he stopped himself. He wanted to draw this out and make it last all night if possible. He wanted to explore every delicious inch of her beautiful body, to touch, caress, to love every part, before he made the final plunge into the wonderful depths of her waiting, willing vagina.

Raising himself up on his hands and knees, he surveyed his prize greedily, inhaling sharply as he felt her hands close around his pulsating cock as if she was afraid that he was leaving her. Her fingers were soft and gentle, but she handled the jerking and quivering shaft of his penis with the skill of an expert, pushing the smooth foreskin down as far as it would go and then pulling his penis forward as she tried to force it into the desperately hungry little opening of her cunt. Joe drew in a sharp breath of surprised pleasure as he felt the softness of her pubic hair tease lightly at the exposed tip of his cock, and he helped by moving closer and allowing her to manipulate his throbbing penis as she wanted sliding it torturously back and forth across the moist throbbing button of her clitoris. The sensation was beautiful for both of them and he had to struggle with himself not to give in to the temptation to impale her on his hard cock then and there.

But it was too soon yet, and he managed to hold himself back by a forced exercise of mind over matter. And too, in one distant corner of his lust distorted brain, there was still the desire to punish her just a little for having been so haughty to him that day on the bus. Her surrender, when it came, had to be complete and absolute, and he sensed that maybe she was not yet one hundred percent his. He could enter her now, if he wanted to, but there would be some tiny corner of her soul left untouched and the young man wanted it all. He was going to do this right and he still had a number of things to try before he completed this total erotic act of love. He wanted her to be his completely.

She wanted to be fucked badly, that much was-perfectly obvious. Melanie lay beneath him almost gasping for breath as her long voluptuously soft body writhed with undisguised lust and her fingers gently massaged him, teasing the tiny slit in the end of his penis with one hand while she used the other to play with his heavily swaying balls. Bu he wanted her to remember this night above all others, to have an erotic experience with him which would blot out all the other men who had seared into her captive belly during her seven days as an unwilling prostitute in the brothel. In order to accomplish this purpose, he had to stimulate her until she was virtually screaming with desire. She had to do more than merely accept his penis into the soft loving depths of her cunt, she had to cry out for it! She had to want it more than anything!

Melanie understood none of this, comprehending only the fact that her body was bursting out of control like a runaway car. Her spine seemed to be alive, frantically twisting and bucking as she reared up against her new lover, wrapping her long tapering legs around his buttocks in a desperately yearning attempt to force him into her highly stimulated young body. Everything had changed for her now, she realized. The men who had visited her while she was enslaved at Ruby's had taught her body to react to certain kinds of stimuli and she had learned her lessons well. If she could respond passionately to a man who had pushed the right buttons despite the fact that she hated him, there were no limits to the kind of reaction she could experience in the arms of a man she loved! The door to sexual pleasure had been opened by Gerome, and now she wanted it all at once and her mind was filled with all manner of wildly erotic images and fantasies which she made no effort to drive away this time.

Joe levered up on his muscular arms and looked down on her with something like pity, seeing that she was really ready for him and deciding that it would be simple cruelty to keep her much longer in this desperate condition. There was just one more little test she had to pass, and then he would know, without a doubt, that she was his all the way, forever.

Moving carefully to avoid destroying the delicately submissive mood she was in, he began to inch his way along her slender but full breasted young body, kissing her lingeringly on the mouth as he crawled up until his buttocks rested lightly on the soft twin cushions of her breasts and his body was bent nearly in half. Her eyes were closed now and he wondered if she understood what he was going to ask of her. As he straightened up and looked down, his eyes locked on her parted lips, his long thick cock swung menacingly like the boom on a crane, trembling only inches away from her sensually parted lips.

She'll never go for this, he warned himself, even after a week in a whorehouse! But he was determined to make the try, tormenting himself with the mental picture of his hard pulsating cock plunged into that delicate little mouth. He moved forward another inch, bending "over a little so that the tip of his penis rested directly on her chin. Now there could be no doubt in anyone's mind what he intended to do and Joe braced himself for a cry of protest. The girl opened her mouth, as if to speak, but no protest emerged.

Instead, her tongue snaked out agilely and she stabbed desperately in the direction of his cock, the tip of her tongue flickering tantalizingly across the rubbery surface of the glands. Joe did not require a clearer invitation than this, inching forward again to close the gap between them and inhaling sharply as Melanie began to use her tongue. Licking lewdly back and forth acorss the sensitive nerve endings and then ducking her head forward to enclose the tightly stretched skin of his cock between her ovaled lips, accepting him joyfully into the sanctuary of her mouth. The girl's lips were soft and smooth, forming a tight elastic ring around his hotly jerking cock and Joe could feel her move it around inside of her moist mouth, lashing at him actively while little mewly sounds and hums of passionate acceptance of him rumbled in her throat. His hands stole into her long hair and he pushed into her a little farther as she began to suck him furiously.

This, to him, was the ultimate proof of where they stood with each other and the young man realized with a surge of emotion that if she sucked him until he came, she would be his for good and no other man would ever be able to take her away again. If she made this final sacrifice of her lusting body to him, it would mean that he had conquered her completely and the idea excited him so profoundly that he began to flex his loins in and out of the tight elastic oval formed by her roundly straining lips, watching avidly as his long hardened shaft disappeared back into the vacumn like depths of her throat, he was overjoyed with waves of increasing passion.

Joe would have liked to go on all night like this, if possible, but the stimulation was too intense to last any longer. He could already feel the familiar heat building up frantically in his testicles and the tension in his loins became more unbearable by the moment.

There was a sudden spasm which raced through his lean aching body and he knew that nothing in heaven or earth could stop him now. He gripped Melanie's head tightly as he began to cum powerfully into her eagerly sucking mouth, pouring the hot sticky sperm from deep in his lusting balls far into the-back of her throat. A low groan of pure sweet ecstasy escaped Melanie's tightly clasping lips as the spray of fiery hot cum spurted wetly into the cavity of her mouth, mixing with the saliva until tiny droplets overflowed her lips and trickled down over her chin in tiny little rivulets. Her throat muscles worked frantically as she gulped this lust inciting fluid, welcoming it into her body as if it were the gift of the gods.

Then it was Joe's turn to moan as he felt the last heated drops of his maleness flood into her wildly working mouth, knowing that it was now over for him, at least for awhile. It had been so good, but so terribly short! But Melanie quite clearly had her own ideas about it being over.

Never removing his limp, slowly deflating instrument from her cum covered lips, she licked it tenderly savoring every tiny pungent drop, caressing his cock with her mouth until the organ began to once again jerk and palpitate, obligingly filling up again with blood and returning it promptly to its original hardness of but a few moments ago. Only when she was certain that she had restored him to the full turgid state of erection did she allow him to remove it from the confines of her mouth, a thin string of semen still connecting her lips to the tip of his throbbing instrument.

"I'm all yours, dearest, do anything you want," she murmured as Joe slid quickly down into position.

The surprised young man wasted no time in taking advantage of this offer, finding that her openly flowering vagina was totally ready. Without a moment's hesitation, he fucked into her, groaning with pleasure as he felt the powerful internal muscles of her cunt throbbing in desperate anticipation. He lost no time in unnecessary foreplay since he recognized that this sweet young girl would never be more ready if she lived another century, and he quickly skewered up inside of her with one hotly searing stroke which carried his rigidly throbbing rod of flesh all the way from the pink -rimmed lips of her tender vagina to the sensitive resistant flesh of her cervix. The smoothing clasping walls of her cunt clung to him like warm honey and the youth nearly went out of his mind with pure delight.

He began fucking in and out of her with long, lust arousing strokes, Melanie's whole body seemed to rise of the bed into him, writhing and gyrating against him as if a powerful electric current were being passed steadily through her excited body, and he squirmed down into her with all the force in him, putting every muscle in his strong muscular body behind each relentless forward lunge.

"Oh, darling, it's so good, so good," she sang to him mindlessly as he filled her with his rock hard penis.

Then, he knew that the release she had been crying for was not far off, so he rose up on his elbows, anxious to watch her face when it came. Lewd wet smacking sounds vibrated through the room as he slammed into her again and again, each quickening thrust bringing her closer to the ultimate goal, her orgasm. It was then that he felt her body grow in it's urgency to bring him even deeper into her desirous cunt and she was reaching that climax that had been denied her for so long. Her legs climbed up to his back and she held onto him with all the strength in her tormented body, moaning for him to never stop. Joe felt himself being propelled into another erotic spewing of his hot cum into her and then they were both in the throes of the most fantastic orgasm of their lives.

It must have lasted an eternity and when they had relaxed back together, arms around one another, on the bed they both were completely satiated having found each other at last!

"Joe, that was the most wonderful thing that ever happened to me," Melanie whispered.

"My pleasure, ma'm ... anytime...." he smiled at her in the soft light. "Melanie?"

"Hummm?" she said sleepily.

"I want you always to be right beside me like this," he said. "But Joe, why?"

"Because you, young lady for the best piece of tail I have ever known, and I can't let you go now," he responded.

"Silly! But Joe, seriously, all of those other men, won't they always be between us?" Hoping when she said it, that she already knew the answer.

"Shhh-the reason I can't let you go is because I love you," he said gently and held her closer in his arms.

THE END

Printed in Great Britain
by Amazon

39581339R00056